Letters
from an
Alien Schoolboy

EARTHLINGS, PLEASE PAY ATTENTION. *This is a cosmic book. Open it at random. Select a word within ten lines from the top and within the first ten words of that line.* MAKE A NOTE OF IT. *Then double the number of that page, multiply the result by five, add thirty, add the number of the line you selected, add five, multiply by ten, add the number of the word in the line, take away three hundred and fifty, and the remainder will give you the page number, line and word in that order (sorry about this Rokbumme, but it is the sort of thing Earthlings find awfully brainy).*

To Lenny Bruce

First published in Great Britain in 2010 by
Piccadilly Press Ltd, 5 Castle Road, London NW1 8PR
www.piccadillypress.co.uk

Text and illustration copyright © Ros Asquith, 2010

Cover and text designed by Simon Davis

ISBN: 978 1 84812 094 5
1 3 5 7 9 10 8 6 4 2

Printed in the UK by
CPI Bookmarque Ltd, Croydon CR0 4TD

Mixed Sources
Product group from well-managed
forests and other controlled sources
www.fsc.org Cert no. TT-COC-002227
© 1996 Forest Stewardship Council
FSC

LETTERS from an ALIEN SCHOOLBOY

TRANSLATED
FROM ALIEN BY
PROFESSOR
R. L. ASQUITH

PICCADILLY PRESS • LONDON

EARTHLINGS BEWARE!

IF YOU SEE THIS SIGN, FOLLOW IT AT YOUR PERIL

FREE ICE CREAM!

Any flavour you like plus fudge sauce and choc f late!

ESPECIALLY IF IT SAYS ANY FLAVOUR YOU LIKE

MISSION EARTH: DAY ONE SUNDAY

Measly Dwelling
Row of Identical Dwellings
Tiny 'Country' Called England
Misshapen Islands Called Britain
Insignificant Dot Called Earth
Feeble Solar System
Forty-third Galaxy from the Right
Virgo Supercluster
Wrong End of the Universe

Dear Rokbumme,

Here we are squashed inside a repulsive 'house' on the most ill-tempered, ugly planet in the Universe – Earth. The weather is grey and freezing, which is not surprising since Earth has only one sun, and that seems to be covered up most of the time with wet floating blobs called 'clouds'.

I am as cold as a *ploogle* and as cross as a bagful of *scratchflackets*.

We arrived here unsafely, nearly beheading two ancient Earthlings, which was all the pilot's fault.

Our unsafe arrival

Flyzoop crossed eighty-two galaxies on the way here without once watching where he was going. It's amazing we got here at all.

We were all trying to relax in the spacecraft's comfort zone, and make the most of our last few days as Faathings before we had to put on our Earth disguises. We were eating the remains of a toasted *flaaark* we'd picked up at that fuel station just to the left of the Crab Nebula, playing pong-ping, flexing our suckers and twirling our antennae – when dozy old Flyzoop screamed,

'METEOR ATTACK! FIRE ALL MISSILES!'

Me and my sister Farteeta looped over to the vision zone and there it was – a huge blue meteor heading straight for us! Our in-flight robot, Bertiolboomflinglebuntusdyoliusfloopfloop (I'll just call him Bert from now on) went mental.

'That's not a meteor, that's Earth you *************!'* he said. 'And it's not heading for US, WE'RE heading for IT.'

Bert rolled down the central aisle, smashing up all the seating and ripping our pong-ping net to shreds. I've never seen him move so fast. He tore the controls out of Flyzoop's suckers and zapped all twelve *ABORT* buttons. Too late – one missile had already launched. We watched it zooming towards Earth.

'That's our mission finished before it's begun,' said Papa.

It turned out Flyzoop's aim is as hopeless as his piloting. The missile shot past Earth and exploded on an even more insignificant dot called Pluto.

'I don't think Pluto is inhabited,' said Papa. 'At least, not by intelligent life as we know it. But then neither is Earth.'

* Editor's note: This book may be read by younglings. Please insert the word 'nincompoop'.

'ANTI-GRAVITY BLASTERS ON! ACTIVATE ANTI-MATTER SHIELDS! INITIATE REPULSION MAGNET! MOBILISE HOVER MODE!'

Bert was a blur of flashing lights and robot arms spinning in all directions. It was just as well we'd brought him with us, because Flyzoop was crouching in the cockpit with his suckers covering all seventeen eyeballs and moaning, 'We're going to *die*! I want my mums.'

Earth hurtled closer – a horrible sight.

'Back in the days of the Eighth and Ninth Quadratic Wars there were real pilots, who could land a burning battle cruiser even if two of their heads and most of their arms had been shot off,' said Papa. 'But this *flurfling* apology for a pilot even forgot to switch on the anti-matter shields!'

He messaged back to Faa: *Mission aborted. We are about to die. Goodbye.*

Mama and Farteeta looped about uselessly. Pluke and I helped Bert, because I am brave, as a true Faathing should be, and because Pluke is my noble pet who would lay down his life for me.

We managed to activate the Hover Mode just four metres from Earth's surface, and the hover blades missed the ancient Earthlings by 0.2 centimetres and set light to a bunch of 'trees' (unfriendly green vegetables, not a bit like the chatty *urqflurbles* in which you and I first learned to climb back home on Faa.) None of us could find the memory-blaster in time to wipe the memories of the two old Earthlings, but luckily for us, once the anti-matter shields were up, we became invisible, so it didn't matter how much they shouted and screamed about an alien attack, because no other Earthlings believed them.

So now we've transformed into our Earthling disguises and are 'settling in' to our unpleasant

ALIENS attacked us!

Yes, yes. Have a nice cup of tea

My bag was swallowed by a BLACK HOLE!

It was a manhole

dwelling. All you can see from its portholes are rows of identical dwellings and grey 'streets'.

The first message from home was your mindscan of me and Pluke on Faa just before I left.

Thanks for that, although it makes my hearts ache to look at it.

See? Back on Faa, even my sad face looks happy.

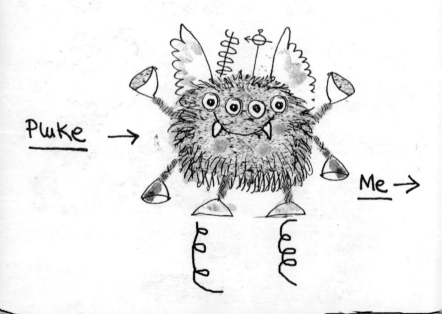

Puke →

Me →

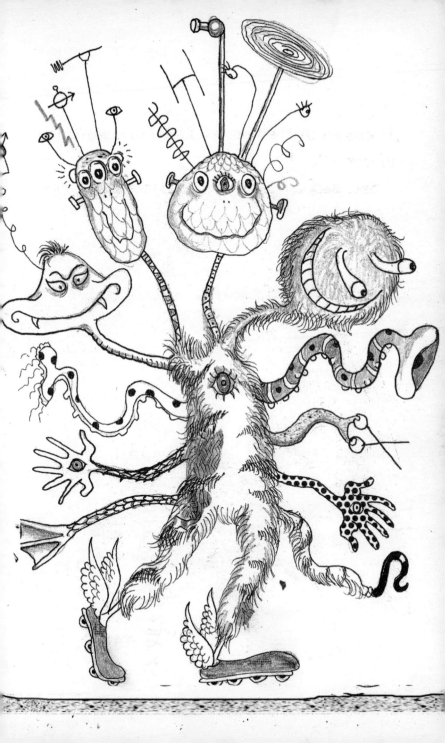

Now I look like this.

So you see the awful truth – *Earthlings have only one head.* No wonder they're so stupid.

And just two eyeballs. And those face *forwards*.

Earthlings start out in life less equipped than our most primitive *fluits* but think they're the most advanced species in the Universe.

I'm supposed to be here, looking like this, for a whole Earth *month*.

School 'Cap'

Hairstyle

Beak

This is my 'smile'. Behind it, my hearts are breaking

'Blazer'

Uni-Jointed 'arms' and 'legs'

Only two grippers

Earthlings are such softies they must protect their 'feet' with two layers: 'socks' and 'shoes'

I have to wear a striped necklace called a 'tie'.

And I have to wear tubes and flaps called 'clothes'.

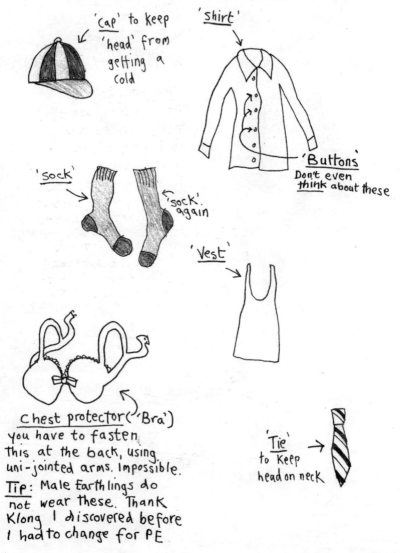

'Cap' to keep 'head' from getting a cold

'Shirt'

'Buttons'
Don't even _think_ about these

'sock'

'sock'. again

'Vest'

Chest protector ('Bra')
you have to fasten this at the back, using uni-jointed arms. Impossible.
Tip: Male Earthlings do not wear these. Thank Klong I discovered before I had to change for PE

'Tie'
to keep head on neck

'Underpants'
There is only one of
these, so why don't
they call it an
'underpant?'
Tip: If you ever come
to Earth, Klong forbid,
make sure you do not
wear the above.
Wear these instead,
 they are called
'Boxers' after
Earthling warriors.

'Shorts' place on
top of 'underpants'
(why?)

'Belt'
Joins 'legs'
to 'body'

'shoe'

Other 'shoe'

Earthlings can't grow fur like us. A lot of other creatures on their planet can, but Earthlings look down on them as inferior.

You've no idea how awful it is here, Rokbumme. Just think – you wake up in the morning expecting everything to be the same as usual, ready to unfold your aerials, give the old heads a bit of a scratch, rub your seventeen eyeballs . . . Then you realise you've got to say goodbye to normality because you're not yourself any more, you're a freak with just one head, two eyeballs, four limbs and no aerials at all. Sounds like a nightmare, doesn't it? Only it's real life!

But that's only the beginning. Then you've got to 'get dressed'.

The instruction manuals are useless.

You should have seen me the first time I tried to put clothes on – trousers over head, on both arms, on legs upside down, you name it. I even had the

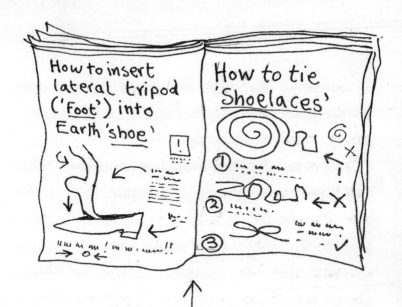

Our instruction Manuals for 'getting dressed' are Very Confusing. It took me Six Earth hours to put on a sock.

underpants-over-the-head in the trousers-upside-down phase.

What a waste of time! You could visit the Pleiades for a game of *snaaark*, stop off to download an encyclopaedia or two at the Infinite Knowledge Base by the Timeless Labyrinths' burger bar, and even drop by Aqua Orbius 9 for a quick swim before breakfast, in the time it takes to get dressed here.

Mama and Papa have given me an Earth name – Hoover Bogey Nigel Custard Toilet Hercules Namby Pamby Harmonica Hedgehog Coldplay Bugspray CroMagnon Colander Junior. I like it, but Papa says he thinks it might be best if Earthlings just call me 'Nigel'. They did a check on all the books written about Earthlings by the cleverest humans, averaged out all the names given to the human species, and threw in a couple of other randomly selected names as wild cards. So that's what I ended up with.

Poor little Pluke has had the worst of the deal – his Earth disguise is that of a horrible smelly human pet called a 'dog'.

He has to run up and down with his mouth drooling spit, cough all the time when he isn't ill (they call it 'barking' here, but it's just the same) and drop waste products all over the place. The sound Pluke makes is like *oozles* mating, and it goes like this:

WERF, **WERF.**

Pluke's Earth name is Rhubarb. I am beginning to wish I hadn't begged Papa to bring him, he looks so sad.

My annoying little sister Farteeta is furious because she has to be an Earthling toddler called Sultana Toilet Hercules Namby Pamby Harmonica Hedgehog Coldplay Bugspray Cro-Magnon Colander, but wants another name too.

'IT'S NOT FAIR! I WANT TO BE CALLED NIGEL!'

Tomorrow I have to start my own special mission – going to a 'school' to collect Earthlings for Papa. Remember that collection of *flonkblatters* I used to have, and you used to ask why I bothered to collect such a low form of life? Well, eat your words, Rokbumme my old friend. *Flonkblatters* could stand on all their heads at once, blow stuff out of their beaks in an interesting range of colours, perform brain surgery on each other, and a quontillian other things. It isn't like that with Earthlings – they do nothing worth studying at all.

Still, all is not lost for them, because now they're about to be Improved, and that's why I have to collect them.

Papa's machine for Improving Earthlings is amazing. And Papa says it can do other top secret things that only he and the Emperor's Secretive Services know about.

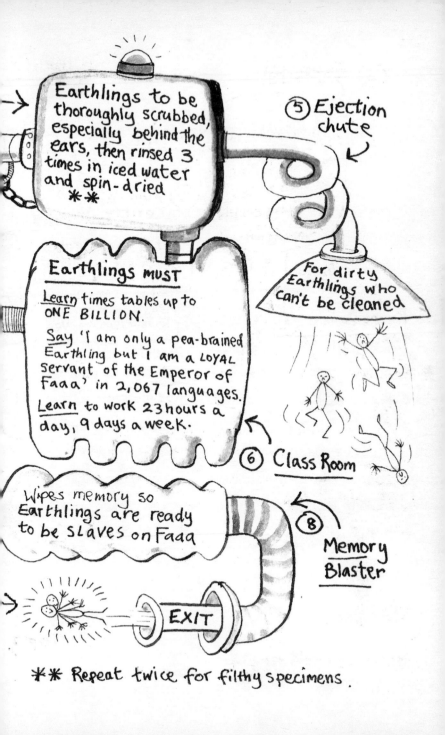

When Farteeta saw the Improver she asked, 'Will it hurt?'

'Not much,' said Papa. 'Earthlings don't have feelings like we do – either physical or emotional. They can't even look happy and furious simultaneously. They're hardly more intelligent than our pets.'

Pluke started barking so hard at this insult that his dog form began to dissolve. We'll have to be careful about this – there's a primitive brain confusion Earthlings get here called 'stress'. It seems to affect us too. Stress and excitement cause problems with our disguises. Anyway, Pluke's four eyeballs had appeared and his springs were growing back – he looked very happy, let me tell you – before we gave him a drink of *Vom*. (Thank *Klong* for *Vom*, the transforming liquid we must always carry in case our disguises slip.) It really won't do if we get discovered just because Pluke has no mental discipline.

'Do Earthlings get the free ice cream at the end?' said Farteeta.

'Of course not,' replied Papa, smiling.

'And what happens when they go down the ejection chute? Do they blow up?'

'Good question,' said Papa. 'They will probably scream very loudly, but I don't think they will explode. Anyway, there are plenty more of them – this planet is very overpopulated. There are 6,934,171,924 people here now.'[*]

[*] *The Earthling population goes up by one every second. So now it will be 6,934,171,932.*

Papa was frowning at his Universe population calculator. He gave it a whack. 'Hmmm. That's very high. Either this is wrong or we're in a different year.'

'It's all very well for you with your Improvers and calculators. I've got to iron the teacups!' Mama shouted, brandishing a long pole.

'That's not an iron, that's a broom,' sighed Papa, consulting his copy or Professor McSquared's *Guide to Earth*.

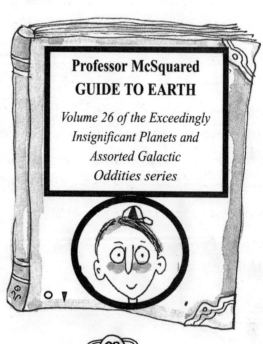

Professor McSquared
GUIDE TO EARTH

Volume 26 of the Exceedingly Insignificant Planets and Assorted Galactic Oddities series

This is the Earthling I based my 'look' on →

'That *querfling* McSquared,' he fumed. 'He's good on imperial dynasties, worm-holes, dark matter, hyper-maths, even Earth clothes for some reason, but he only gives two pages to all this stuff about teacups and irons and pillows, because he's just not interested in it.'

'Typical professor – hasn't a clue what a kitchen's for,' Mama said, as if she had the slightest idea herself. She hates the idea of being an Earth 'housewife' because apparently they're supposed to spend all day cleaning and flattening clothes. Normally she would be fanning herself in a nice pool of *aquanium*, ordering the slaves about, and now she has to do everything for herself – how exhausting. But here, we have to follow the Rules (*Interplanetary Health and Safety Guide to Exploring Other Planets*, p.981) and live as Earthlings do. But it is only half a life, Rokbumme. No – a quadzillionth of a life.

Even our month's training didn't prepare us for spending a whole day squashed together in a tiny 'house' as a 'family'. There is no space to whirl or loop. Frankly, I would rather spend a day *flooshple-blooping* than spend another day here.

And tomorrow, it's school. My task this week, Rokbumme, is to make a friend and lure him home 'for tea' so Papa can try out his Improver. If it works OK, then Papa's going to Improve all Earthlings, by making them cleverer. He says their feeble systems couldn't stand being boosted up to our level of intelligence, but he thinks they can be enhanced by a factor of one hundred. This should make them understand the errors of their ways so that they will stop fighting the World War and therefore have peace on Earth. Papa says even deadly dull planets like Earth should be saved if possible, to preserve the 'bio-diversity of the Universe'. If the mission works, then Papa will get a medal from the

Intergalactic Secretive Services Committee presented by the Emperor himself! We'll bring a few of the very best Earthlings back as slaves, too, so we'll never have to *bloople* a *flooshple* ever again.

Bert came into my room earlier, bleeping and buzzing. He has got a room to himself, but he isn't settling. He is even more lonely than us, with no robots to talk to and nothing within a quadzillion light years with a brain like his. He says he has been having visions of Threggs. Remember how your great-great-great grandpa gave us nightmares describing their oily purple faces? And how he told us they liked to eat sweet little Hunnybeams, the kindest creatures in all the galaxies? Threggs can't even digest Hunnybeams, they just enjoy seeing their little legs waving about. But I've been reading about Threggs and they're even worse than I thought.

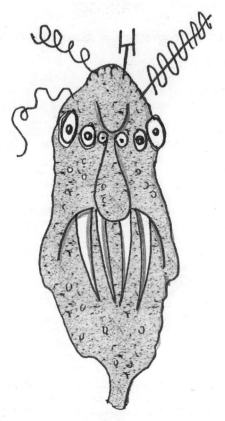

Thregg: *Defeated by brave and noble Faathings in the Sixth Quadratic Wars.*

Papa says this shows a Thregg looking HAPPY. Why? He has just consumed 40 kilos of spinach and 25 HUNNYBEAMS

THREGGS

Most destructive species in the Universe. Nastier than Klygons and Slxxgkpqrs combined but less subtle.

Colour: Purple with small turquoise pustules. Beige underbelly, pink overbelly.

Limbs: Forty-five posterior tentacles, sixty-eight anterior tentacles.

Heads: Singular.

Brain: Singular, therefore minimal.

Vision: Moderate (six frontal eyeballs, twin rear periscopes).

Velocity: Maximum.

Strength: Considerable.

Hearing: Acute. (Used the Noisy Neighbours legislation of the Second Quadratic period to justify their destruction of adjacent galaxies.)

Habits: Indescribable (see adults only section, p.9400).

Other notes: Addiction to spinach, an edible flowering vegetable. Once common, now almost extinct. Still prolific on only five small planets: Gleriz-boccoboppalus 20, DR2zz, Plim, Quaquaquoque, Thrubb. And, possibly, Earth.

I reminded Bert that we defeated the Threggs way back in the Sixth Quadratic Wars, before he was even a microchip, which seemed to calm him down. I think we made a mistake when we programed Bert to have feelings.

Talking of which, I'm really missing Mum and Dad, as well as Mummy and Daddy and Mother and Father, although don't tell them or they'll think I'm not noble and brave. It is weird being here with only two parents and my most annoying sister. But that is how lots of Earthlings live.

Your friend
till *flooshples*
learn
self-respect,
Flowkwee

By the way, the second most evil species after Threggs look like this

So you cannot always judge by appearances

MISSION EARTH: DAY TWO MONDAY

Dear Rokbumme,

A day of unpleasant surprises!

It seems we got our Earth dates wrong by approximately 2,207,520,000 seconds. This means we have not arrived in the Earth year of 1942, as we thought, and that the World War has been over for nearly seventy Earth years. The ludicrous little island called Britain that we've ended up on, somehow won it – the other army must have become weak with laughing, and fallen into a black hole by accident.

Adolf Hitler, the small, shouting man with a furry lip, is long dead. Apparently he thought one kind of Earthling was much better than other kinds, and so had much more right to live than all the rest. Since it's obvious to anyone with half a *flaaarnn* working that all Earthlings are exactly the same (except for a few minor differences of shape, colour and furriness) and all of them equally ridiculous, this Hitler was clearly completely mad.

Mama took me and Farteeta for our first day at school today. Of course, we are not going to the same school – Farteeta is just going to a horrid little pen called a playgroup. Mama pushed us in a big box on wheels called a 'pram', which we kept falling out of. It was awful fitting into it with Farteeta kicking and squawking like a *spittoon*, but it was worse when I realised that I am definitely the wrong age and size to be in a pram. Even Farteeta is too old.

We got some strange looks on the way to school, but when we got there our mistake was obvious – the parent-Earthlings just raised those beastly furry lines way up above their eyeballs, but the younglings all started making rude remarks and laughing.

'Laughing' is an unpleasant, creaking, Earthling reaction to something called a 'joke'. I don't really get this, but jokes seem to be largely about space/time miscalculations – like falling over, treading in dog poo-poos and bumping into solid objects.

But back to school. I stood up when the teacher, Miss Barn, came in and shouted 'Salve, Magister'. In Professor McSquared's book, it said Latin was a language spoken by a successful Earthling racial type called the Romans. Well, maybe, but it's *fnooks* to him. Nobody speaks Latin here now, and you just get the laughing noise if you try it. So learning Latin was a whole hour wasted.

Turn the Angry Teacher upside down to see the Naughty Laughing Boy. (Earthlings do not respect Teachers as we do.)

Earthlings have no respect for their teachers and do not stand up when they come into the room, like it tells you to in the *Guide*. Earthlings seem to think teachers are 'jokes' which may explain their slow development.

Nobody was wearing Professor McSquared's 'school uniform' either. They wear clothes in different colours, which does mean it's slightly easier to tell Earthlings apart, but not much.

Remember how we screamed when we first looked at pictures of aliens in Year One Universe studies? Well, Earthlings are uglier than *any* of them, even Threggs. They are utterly bald without patterns or fur except for a scrap on top, which they call a hairstyle. Their body colour is grey with yellowish, brownish or pinkish shades, like underheated *zardles* or over-cooked *zooks*. And because they have no aerials, sensors, lights, propellers, whirlers or winkers they cannot loop, zoom or even fly.

And the smell! I had to wear the invisible beak muffler all day.

They do, however, have smell-sensors like us. They are tubes encased in a protective beak attached to the front of their single head. The efficiency of these beaks is almost totally neutralised by *glopulous* obstructions called 'bogeys'.

BOGEYS!!!!
EARTHLING
ALERT
THE PUBLISHER
HAS BANNED
THIS PICTURE OF BOGEYS
SAYING IT IS TOO DISGUSTING
FOR YOUNGLINGS.
SORRY.

I'm furious because I am the smallest in my class. Why did Papa get the measurements wrong? If I was my real height I'd be four Earth metres tall.

Today I learned that Earthling knowledge amounts to less than the most infinitesimal, minuscule, microscopic, pathetiscopic speck of zilch in the vast Everythingness of the Universe. The place is a waste of space. They don't know how many stars there are in the Milky Way which is their own galaxy. They don't know that there are ten thousand galaxies in only 0.000024 percent of their sky. Or even how many countries there are on their own Earth. Or why one and one isn't always two. They have no idea that they are made of only three particles. And they use dictionaries in their *own language*. Even in this country, they don't know all the words there are in English! (Extraordinary, because they only use twenty-six letters, so the number of possible combinations is tiny.) It is difficult to pretend to be as dumb as them.

I kept putting my gripper up to answer Miss Barn's questions and every answer was right. The class didn't like it, and said I was 'posh', and 'talked like Prince Charles'.

Then Miss Barn asked us to spell various words including 'spinach', a pleasant looking vegetable that you may remember the evil Threggs are addicted to, but which all the Earthlings hate. I

put up my
gripper
again and –
SQUILLOONS
– my top
right sucker
appeared out of
the sleeve of my clothes-
tube! My disguise was
wearing off! Maybe it was
because I was stressed
thinking about Threggs.

There was a long silence,
except for a few scared
breathing noises. Then the
laughing became so loud that
all my heads throbbed, but I
managed to swig some *Vom*
secretly before any of them

became visible. My sucker shot back into my sleeve.

Miss Barn went a grisly shade of green (like your great-great-great granny, no offence) before saying, 'Most amusing, Nigel, but this is a classroom, not a joke shop. Stay back after the lesson.'

Miss Barn is enormous and flabby with a huge beak. The bogeys in there must be the size of the Crab and Fingoogle Nebulae put together. I put my cap on in case I was sprayed with any of them.

All the other Earthlings filed out at the end of the lesson, looking at me as if I was an alien.

Little do they know!

Miss Barn did some smiling at me, but it's a lot different to our smiling at home. As you know, we turn the corners of our mouths up at different angles on different heads, so Head One might be completely happy while Head Two is a little puzzled but feeling quite warm, Head Three says you seem quite nice, and so on. Out of all these

Miss Barn's bogey eruption. Earthlings
call it a 'sneeze'

signals, we process the feelings involved and know what to do. But Earthlings show only one feeling at a time. It's not surprising they have so many wars.

'I know it's your first day, Nigel,' Miss Barn was saying, 'but making silly jokes isn't really a way to win friends and influence people.'

'I apologise for my wrongdoings and will be happy to stay in detention and write out however many lines you wish me to,' I said (just like it told us to in the *Guide*). As I left, I heard Miss Barn muttering that I was 'such a nicely spoken boy'.

When I got back home, I found that Papa had realised we had the date wrong, and had spent all day reading the *History of Earth Since World War Two*. I told him I was worried I'd never make a friend for the Improver because everyone said I was posh, and talked like Prince Charles.

'Prince Charles is going to be the next King of

England,' Papa said, looking at the index. 'So there's nothing bad in talking like him. But Posh is a female married to someone called David Beckham, a Master Kicker of Balls.'

I was about to ask why this skill has made the Earthling Beckham very famous when we were interrupted by Farteeta screaming upstairs,

'Help! MONSTER!'

We zoomed up and found her shaking and weeping beside a terrible roaring, gurgling beast.

'I just shook its hand!' wailed Farteeta. 'Now it's gushing and spitting at me.'

Papa fired three shots from his stun laser at the brute, which exploded, and water flooded the room.

Mama looped in screeching, 'You've smashed the toilet you half-witted ******!'*

Editor's note: As I have pointed out before, this book may be read by younglings. Please insert the word 'baboon'.

Well, that was the worst surprise so far.

I will write about this in very small letters so it will seem less upsetting.

Earthlings do poo-poos. Just like our pets do. But they don't go outside and dig a hole, they do it in a little furniture called a toilet. INSIDE their own homes.

They are so primitive, Rokbumme, that they don't even digest all the food they eat!

At least it doesn't matter that Papa smashed the toilet because none of us will need it.

'There, there, Farteeta,' said Mama. 'I meant to explain it to you, but I didn't want to tell you everything at once because I thought you would be too frightened to come.' Then she whispered to herself, 'And there are much worse things than that.'

'Shhh,' said Papa. 'You don't want to give her nightmares.' Papa had been too bored to read about houses and so he'd left that up to Mama. But even he was shocked by the poo-poos. He had four spoons

of *Koma* to steady his nerves. However, it didn't work – he wobbled about and fell downstairs, using language I haven't heard before. (I don't know if we'll ever get used to stairs. Earthlings need them for everything, even getting on and off streets.)

So now I am folded up in my agonising Earth bed. The Health and Safety Rule says that we have to sleep as Earthlings do in case a burglar discovers us. It is painful lying down flat – I wish I was back home, hanging upside down from an *urqflurble*. But apparently the only things that sleep that way on Earth are little creatures called bats[*], which means 'mad', so we're not allowed.

[*] Bats, I have now discovered, are quite intelligent compared to humans. Earthlings can't hear a word they say (the frequency is too high), but I tuned into them last night. Bats are plotting to take over the Earth, helped by a highly organised species called ants and charming water mammals called dolphins. This would be an improvement. It also shows upside down sleeping is better for brains.

At least I have some hot water bottles, which is how Earthlings keep warm at night. We have seventeen bottles each, which means Mama has to boil sixty-eight kettles of water to fill them.

I keep wondering what Mama meant. What could possibly be worse than doing poo-poos in your own house? And what will our mission be now there's no World War to stop and we can't bring peace on Earth? I know Earthlings are always fighting little wars which we could clear up, but I have a feeling Papa has some other mission that he isn't telling us about. If so, what is it? And what will I do if the class asks to see my sucker?

If I don't survive, please look after Pluke.

Some hot water bottles → have furry covers.

Oh, and Farteeta. And some are disguised as pets ↘

Maybe.

Your friend,

Flowkwee

Dear Rokbumme,

Dressed in normal clothes today, which Papa organised for 'leisure wear': a pale pink shirt covered in flowering vegetables and a pair of shiny violet trousers with turquoise spots, which reminded me of Threggs. It still took me ages to get into them.

I'm having serious doubts about Papa's ability to direct our mission. I mentioned the spinach spelling incident yesterday and he went mental.

'Spinach? Spinach grows here? Are you sure?' he

kept saying. Then this morning he was trying to understand some strange data Bert had given him, and he was using all four heads, which is against the Rules.

I asked him what was the matter, and he guiltily retracted his extra brains and shook his one sad Earth head. 'It's something on the scanners. They haven't worked out what it is back home,' he said, 'but it's big and it's going fast. It's just passed the Seyfert's Sextet galaxies. It's 190 million light years away, but they still think it could get close to this feeble little solar system within a few Earth days.'

'Could it be a meteor that will blow up Earth?' I asked hopefully.

'It could be. But Flyzoop's on standby, orbiting Neptune, so he'll see it first and tell us. We'd still get off in time.'

So that's OK, because I can't wait to get off this measly wreck of a planet. But I might as well tell you, I also heard Papa muttering, 'But it might be something worse.' Well, *Klong* knows what could be worse than a giant meteor . . .

Unless it's 'literacy hour', which we had at school today, along with 'maths', 'art' and 'P.E.'.

In literacy hour I tried to read like a newborn baby (Papa's advice) to avoid arousing suspicion, but Miss Barn put me in the fast readers' group anyway. So I am in a group called Moles (moles are a blind sub-species that burrow in mud). The ones who can't read are in a group called Lions – which are noble creatures that all other animals including Earthlings are scared of.

I put up my gripper and asked, 'Why is the top clever group given a measly name and the slow-witted, idiotic buffoons are named after the King of the Jungle?'

Miss Barn said I wasn't being very kind. Why?

The boy sitting next to me said I was 'wicked'.

So obviously he hates me. It makes me feel a bit funny to think that. This boy is a bit less ugly than most Earthlings, with quite a little turned-up beak without too many bogeys and lots of ribbons on his head. He's called Susan.

Susan, a fine fellow

I tried to write badly and spell wrong, but Miss Barn put a smiley face on my work anyway and Susan said I was wicked again. I was determined to do worse at maths, so people would like me. When Miss Barn asked if I knew my nine times table I very cleverly lied saying, 'I only know up to two million and six times nine.'

It turns out they only do multiplication tables up to times-ten. We are only just discovering how thick these Earthlings really are.

Art was weirdest of all. You make a picture that can be of something you see in your head! It doesn't even have to be of anything real! You use runny messy colours called 'paint'.

I don't know why they bother to do this, Rokbumme, because for them, colours are just a mixture of red, yellow and blue. They only have three kinds of light-sensors in their measly two eyeballs, so no infra-red, no ultra-violet, no *oravalooom* or *muoniblat*!! They go mental over rainbows – simple, dull bands of parallel stripes caused by refraction of their weedy sun's rays by rain.

Anyway, Miss Barn told us to make a picture of something we liked. I thought it would be fun to do Susan, but looking as if he liked me rather than as if he thought I was wicked.

The class all started making their pictures. It was sad to watch them. They made a line, then rubbed it out, then made a circle and put sticks on it, and pretended it was their mum. They got colours all over the paper and all over themselves and stuck their 'tongues' out in crossness. (Tongues – don't get me started. Gross.)

I don't know how this happened, Rokbumme, but before I knew it, my right sucker shot out of my sleeve, two grippers I wasn't supposed to have sprang out from under my jacket, and I drew Susan's features with the sucker, holding a thing called a 'pencil', and filled in as many of his colours as I could with the grippers using the brushes and paints.

It was all over in much less than the time it took Susan to draw a beak in the middle of a circle. Luckily for me, Rokbumme, Earthlings really are nearly blind and very slow-sighted, so no one noticed. (The only animals on Earth who have vision speed anything like us are adorable clever little creatures called 'flies', which Earthlings hate. I suppose they are jealous.)

Flies. Delightful friendly creatures with excellent vision.

'Art is jolly spiffing,'* I told Miss Barn, trying to make up for the Moles and Lions error. 'We never did this at my last school.'

Miss Barn gave me a very pitying look as if my whole family had been vapourised. 'You never did any painting, Nigel? You poor little soul.'

Then Miss Barn looked at my picture and sat down.

'This is very naughty of you, Nigel. You secretly brought this portrait of Susan into class, and now you're trying to pretend you painted it. That's cheating.'

Susan was staring hard at me. 'No, he didn't, Miss Barn,' Susan said. 'I just saw him do it. Look, the paint's still wet.'

Miss Barn felt the paint, looked at me, then at

* I haven't heard anybody else say 'jolly spiffing' yet, by the way, so I'm beginning to wonder if this is another of Professor McSquared's little calendar-miscalculations.

the picture, then back at me, then at Susan. 'In that case, you're a genius!' she said.

The class all went,

'Wooooooooooooooo.'

Miss Barn wanted to talk to me about it, but it was time for P.E.

On the way to the P.E. place, everyone said I was 'cool' and 'wicked'. These words mean 'cold' and 'evil' in Professor McSquared's dictionary – they obviously all hate me. I wish I hadn't done the picture now.

An especially ugly boy, called Colin Snell, with a horrid yellow hairstyle and frightening blue eyeballs hissed, 'Teacher's pet,' and gave me a kick. I recognised his nasty features – he lives next door to us.

So now I am cold, evil, posh – which means female – and a pet.

Colin started asking me about 'the fat little dwarf in the funny buggy' I came to school with.

'That's my sister. She's wicked,' I told him.

'I've heard she's called Sultana,' Colin said, curling his lip up in a way that didn't look very nice. Everyone laughed like *plongule*s at this.

'No, her name's Farteeta,' I said without thinking. Everyone screeched when I said that. 'But I often call her Farta,' I added. The *plongule* laughing increased by a factor of four decibels. *Klong!* How could I be so stupid as to tell them her real name?!

'No, no, not really, it *is* Sultana,' I said, with my best smile.

'No it isn't, it's Farter! FARTER! FARTER!' they shouted, clapping their hands and jumping up and down.

'Don't do that,' Susan said. 'It's not his fault what his sister's called.'

Maybe Susan likes me a bit after all.

P.E. was the next nightmare, or so I thought at first. It involves running about, and on only two 'legs' too. We all went out on a small rectangle of short green vegetables called 'grass'. The teacher, Mr Grimes, threw us a bouncing sphere, or 'ball', to kick around and try to steal from each other using our 'feet'.

I quickly realised that this is our own traditional game of *fatool*, sometimes known as *sucker orbs*, as originally devised by the legendary warrior race of Goonathons on the low-gravity planet Reff in the minus-quadrupleth century. But here they play it with only one ball because they live in just three dimensions, and because they can't skim or zoom and are without springs, whizzers or buzzers, and can kick with only one foot at a time.

To win, you must kick the ball in between two posts. This is of course a bit different to *fatool*, in

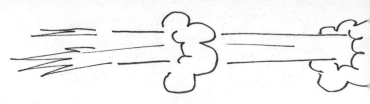

which you kick a dense aggregation of protons down a heavily defended galaxy-wide tube ringed by hyper-magnets, and your score is the mega-tonnage of the resulting nuclear reaction to the nearest squillion.

An Earth goal, unlike a *fatool* one, is so wide that even a newborn *fluit* could kick a ball into it. And that's all you have to do!

They put me at the back near our goal and I was supposed to stop the other team, led by the beastly Colin Snell, from kicking a ball into it. Easy. Colin came towards me with the ball, I stuck out a posterior extender and doubled its length, kicked the ball off Colin's toe, calculated its trajectory and descent, skimmed horizontally to meet it 'on the volley' as they say here, and shot it into their goal off the underside of the crossbar.

It's lucky I am not playing against a team of flies, because they would have spotted these super

speedy movements.

Everyone yelled excitedly, and before I knew it Orville Muffin had kicked the ball to me again. I did a quick mass-times-acceleration and blood-oxygen assessment, locked vision on to Orville, who was running forwards, and kicked the ball along the coordinates.

It knocked Orville Muffin flat into a puddle, *karoomed* between the heads of three of the enemy, and hissed back just in time for its motion to be reversed by the end of my swinging extender.

Something went a bit wrong at this point, because although the ball now maintained its steady ninety miles per Earth hour goalwards and its twelve-degree bend to the left, it picked up four enemy defenders, one behind the other, on the way. They made such a big muddy pile all on top of each other in the goal that in the end, there was

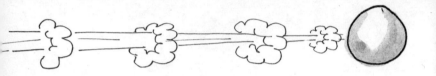

hardly room for the ball to make it over the line. I scored four more easy goals until Mr Grimes, with a funny look at me, blew his whistle.

People on my team were now bashing me on the back and yelling! What had I done wrong this time? Maybe it was because I hadn't let anyone else score.

In the second half of the game I was more careful. I only scored two goals and I made sure I didn't knock anyone over. It was exhausting trying to be so slow and pathetic.

Then everyone started hitting me again, but they were showing me their chewing-blades in what I know is a sign of Earthling friendliness, so maybe it's OK.

Susan was in a different P.E. group, but at the end of the day he came over.

'I heard you scored eight goals,' he said to me.

'Just a lot of *flaarp* – I mean luck,' I said back.

'And you can paint a picture quicker than my phone takes a photo,' he went on. I shrugged, not knowing what this meant.

We were interrupted by Colin Snell bumping into me and shouting, 'My dad's coming round to see your dad later! Yeah! He's mad 'cos your rubbish dog's been playing with our special one! Your dog'll probably have to be taken away!'

Squilloons! Poor Pluke!

But Susan gave me another nice smile, as if he might be able to help.

The Improver should be ready in a few days, and I have to make a friend to Improve. I think Susan might be the one.

I got home to find Papa and Bert fussing away about the approaching Thing. Whenever I try to ask Papa about peace on Earth and our mission, he just says, 'You get on with your part of the mission and let me get on with mine.' But he's not himself,

Rokbumme. I've got a bad feeling about it. There's something he isn't letting on. Let's hope this Thing *is* a meteor, then with a bit of *flaarp* we'll be home soon. Keep your suckers crossed.

Yours in science,
Flowkwee

This is how
Earthlings draw
stars.

And this is how
they draw suns.
Don't they realise
stars and suns are
the same?

Dear Rokbumme,

Papa failed to do his Salute to Our Beloved
Emperor at breakfast! You might think how great
that is, not to have to recite the Emperor's forty
thousand virtues (and one fault, because nobody's
perfect), and if I was back home on Faa, I'd agree.
But for Papa to forget it is bad, bad news. He's
been up two nights running with Bert, frantically
doing calculations, and Bert is not himself at all
either. He hasn't played a single game of
Intergalactic Roulette with me since we arrived, but

barricades himself in his room. All you can hear from there is him burbling about the time it takes to cross the Pisces-Cetus Supercluster Complex. He sends messages to the Secretive Services about the Outer Space Treaty, but you know how it is – they always put you on hold and play one of the Emperor's longest speeches while you're waiting. Then Bert starts cursing his circuits and fizzing. I was about to ask him and Papa some more about it, but the doorbell clanged, and when I looked over the staircase I could see it was the horrible Colin Snell's father from next door.

The Snells have a disgusting little dog-creature named Fi Fi.

Pluke has made friends with it and for some reason they keep running off into the bushes together. He likes Fi Fi better than me, I think.

'Pleased to meet you,' I heard Colin's father say to Mama. Then he said, 'I think my dog's in your

garden,' as he pushed past her into our house. You can see where Colin gets his personality from.

We almost *flooped* into panic mode. There's only one thing in our 'garden' and that's the Improver! Fortunately, Mr Snell shouldn't know it's there, because Papa hid it in a thing called a 'garden shed' which is a kind of nest for Earthling males where Earthling females aren't allowed to go – one

of the few good ideas I've come across down here,
come to think of it.

'I don't want Fi Fi playing with your Rupert,' Mr
Snell was saying.

'Rhubarb,' corrected Mama.

'That's what I said. Anyway, Fi Fi is a pedigree
poodle and I don't want your mongrel getting up
to any tricks with her. Anything could happen.'

What did he mean?

Fi Fi obviously *did* want to play with Pluke, and Mama said she didn't mind if they did. Mr Snell stomped back from the bushes clutching the wriggling, werfing Fi Fi.

'You never got planning permission for that shed,' he said. Fortunately you couldn't see the Improver. 'It's an eyesore. I was hoping for cooperative neighbours, but if this is your attitude . . . '

'Would you like to sit down for a nice glass of sherry? Or a delicious loaf?' asked Mama, repeating some meaningless polite Earthling questions she'd learned from Professor McSquared's book (apparently called 'small talk').

'Got nothing to sit on, have you?' said Mr Snell, looking around our biggest room. 'Maybe this neighbourhood's a bit out of your league. Hope your stuff arrives soon,' he said, laughing a horrible laugh.

'What did he mean about stuff arriving?' said

Mama when he'd gone. 'And an eyesore? It's a *lovely* shed. Well, we'd better order some stuff to arrive, or we'll arouse suspicion.'

So now I have to look up all the stuff Earthlings fill their houses with. What a waste of time. Earthling children like playing games on computers that Bert could out-think even if you unplugged all his memory banks, and they also like 'TV', a box that tells you stories that aren't even true. Not only that, it's just a flat screen in two dimensions, so how could it tell you anything worth knowing?

The 'most popular game on Earth' is *Grand Theft Spacecraft: Invasion* where you have to stop an evil alien horde intent on destroying Earth. I guess that could be quite a fun game if you cared about saving Earth.

There's a whole lot else we're supposed to need – 'chairs', 'tables', 'sofas', 'cupboards'. It's tiring to even think about, especially as the only furnishings we've used so far are beastly beds. Everything else is bound to be as bad. But Mama's found out about 'money', little metal discs, plastic cards and bits of paper that Earthlings are crazy about and use to get things, so she's going to order furnishings. The TV and the computer are coming

Adam 1

Adam 2

Adam 3

Colin Snell →

← Susan

Roddy Asquith

I ♥ MUSIC

first – we get those tomorrow.

Papa's nagging me to choose a friend to test the Improver on. Here's a mind-scan of my class.

Aaron Ratchet

Kanwar

Ben Bingle

Jatinder

Linda

Sophie Tucker

Orville Muffin

Annie Spratt

Emily Binden

Who will I choose? Maybe you can help me. But blur the contrast, or you might be sick.

Your friend till space freezes,
Flowkwee

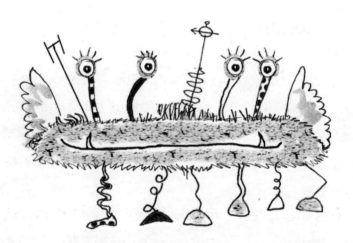

By the way, thanks for this mindscan of Pluke's friend, Skab. I am sorry she is missing Pluke, but I'm afraid he has eyeballs only for FiFi.

MISSION EARTH: DAY FIVE THURSDAY

Dear Rokbumme,

Well, the TV did reveal something interesting – why they all hit me when I scored those goals in football. We watched a football game on TV, and they all do it! It means they like you, not that they hate you!

This means everyone *will* want to be my friend, and there'll be plenty of Earthlings to choose from for the Improver. Heh! Heh! (This is a representation of Earth laughter.)

Thanks for getting back to me so fast about the

mindscan. I agree about Colin Snell – he's the Enemy and could really do with Improving. It's true Orville Muffin isn't bad, but he's been off school since I knocked him into the mud. Aaron Ratchet is too large to get through the door of the garden shed. Ben Bingle's beak runs with water so much he might blow up the electrics. Annie Spratt is always crying, so same problem. Adams One, Two and Three go everywhere together.

But Susan is a good idea. He lent me his eraser today and seems one of the less stupid ones, and that smile he gave me when Colin Snell was doing his Farteeta jokes gave me a strange, nice feeling.

Talking of Farteeta, Papa has banned her from playgroup. Even though she's only three Earth years old, Farteeta is way ahead of all Earthlings her size – but she isn't clever enough yet to know when to keep her one Earth mouth shut. Apparently she started counting and didn't stop at ten, like she's

supposed to. Then she demonstrated a little very basic local geometry (calculating the trajectory of a 'marble run' which she'd assembled in two nano-seconds so the marbles whizzed over the sandpit, looped round the dressing-up corner and dropped *ping, ping, clacketty ping*, straight into the teacher's pocket). Then she asked the nursery nurse why humans thought they were cleverer than flies.

The nursery nurse has apparently been watching her very carefully.

So that was the end of fun for Farteeta. Papa has forbidden her and Mama to leave the house. He is afraid they will give us away. Papa says the Emperor's laws forbidding females from operating heavy machinery or doing complicated tasks are there for a very good reason. He says they don't have the same spatial awareness or strong moral sense as us males. Mama and Farteeta seem to think differently, but Papa is usually right.

Papa is getting more and more agitated. I've never seen him like this before. He keeps asking Bert if there's any more news about the Thing coming across the galaxies towards us, but Bert just gets cross and says, 'INSUFFICIENT DATA!' Bert's still in a foul mood. Instead of making his usual computer noises of bleeping and wheezing and twanging, he goes, 'Spon, speen, spinach!'

As for Papa, I hate to think it, but maybe he's catching an Earthling illness called 'fearfulness'. He's got frightened about us breathing the air because of how dirty Earth is and how it will die soon because Earthlings have warmed it up too much – which is weird, because it's always freezing here. He keeps thinking everything is dangerous and worrying that one of these random metal things called 'cars' will squash me on the way to school. And he's banned us from using the TV, saying it will radiate us and fry our brains. He's also run an interplanetary check on nearby sources of spinach and forbidden Mama to order any even though we're supposed to have some Earth food to offer visitors. Papa needs to get out more.

I wish I was back home with you on Faa, chatting to my *urqflurble*.

Thanks for saying you like my messages and only fell asleep a few times reading them. When I'm writing to my other mamas and papas I only tell them I'm having a wonderful time, because otherwise they worry. You know what mamas and papas are like.

Flowkwee

Dear Mums and Dads,
Having a lovely time.
This is a 'post card'
which Earthlings send
from their 'holidays'.
Isn't it sweet?
I scored 8 goals in
Earthling fatool, but
please don't be cross
as this is an excellent
score for them.
Hail to the Emperor.
Your affectionate
and obedient son
Flowkwee

Earth King
→

Mother, Father, Mum,
Dad, Mummy & Daddy,
Urqflurbles 200,
247, 986.
Pod.
FAA.
Fourbillionth Galaxy to
the left.
Right End of the Universe.

Dear Rok,

Do you mind me addressing you as just 'Rok'? And would it be OK if I sign off as 'Flowk' from now on? I'll tell you about 'bum' and 'wee' when I get back to Faa. Susan told me about them today. Just take my word for it, you don't want to have those words in your name. Not on Earth. Or 'fart', either, come to that. Poor Farteeta.

Today began well with everyone running up and slapping me, saying I was a football star.

'So I am not Posh,' I said, 'I am David Beckham.'

And they all laughed. I think I may have made my first Earth joke.

Of course, now they wanted me to do it all again. Papa said that would happen. These feeble Earthlings love heroes.

'You looked almost like you were flying!' somebody shouted. 'You've got superpowers!' said somebody else.

'I'm just the same as you,' I said to them all. 'Look.' I raised my two useless Earth arms, then rolled up my trousers and showed my stupid knobbly uni-jointed Earth legs. Everyone had a good look, and realised it was true.

'You're a legend, then,' said Aaron Ratchet, bouncing a ball. 'I'll be your manager on an exclusive five-year deal. Show us some keepy uppies.'

He threw me the ball. As you know, Rok, it's child's play to calculate the motions and angles through identical vertical movements of a lower

extender to keep an air-filled spherical object in perpetual motion. After one hundred of them, with the eyeballs of all the class turning as round as the ball, I said, 'Whoever gets this can be on my team.' Then I kicked it over the assembly hall, over the steaming bubbling kitchens, over the playground, and off the far post on the football field into the goal. They all ran screaming after it except for Susan.

'That was pretty good,' he said.

I took a deep breath of the Earth air Papa says is so bad for us, but it helped when I finally asked Susan if he could come to tea. He went a nasty pink colour but made a smiling face and wrinkled up his beak. 'Why me?' he asked.

'Because you're a spiffing fellow. You're not like the other boys.'

Susan giggled (which is a nice, gurgly laugh, like being tickled). 'I should hope not,' he said.

There – I knew he was a fine fellow.

So he is coming to tea tomorrow. And we can try out the Improver. At last, my mission is taking off! Maybe I'll get Space Explorer Level Ten!

The day went downhill from there.

First, there was my lunch box, full of the usual *zardles* and *ming*. I usually eat it quickly so no one sees it, and I can't swap with anybody else because Papa says my stomachs can't digest Earth food. The last thing I want is to have to use the toilet.

I asked Carmel what was in his sandwich and he said 'chicken'.

'But that's a *creature*.'

'Of course a chicken's a creature. Where have you lived all your life? Another planet?'

So there it is. Earthlings eat all those Earth animals we studied at home and thought were their pets:

cows, pigs, lambs, chickens, dogs, cats, beetles, salmon, monkeys, dear little clever flies. Everything.

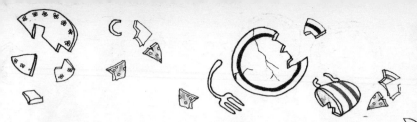

I had to go home early, I felt so sick.

'I know it's a shock,' said Mama. She was trying to work one of the new kitchen furnitures that's for washing things. She had put the cups and saucers in it, but it didn't sound right to me. Pluke and I stood for a while staring through the little window on the front of it while all the things inside whirled round and round, smashing into bits.

'Maybe the machine sticks them all together again once they're nice and clean,' Mama said, frowning an Earth frown. 'Anyway, please don't tell Farteeta about eating the pets. We must try to be understanding of atrocious Earthling habits. They are very simple creatures, I'm afraid.'

But they poo in their own *houses* and they eat their *pets*? How can we *possibly* Improve them when they've got so far to go?

But perhaps the Improver will save Susan from being an Earthling and make him nearly as clever

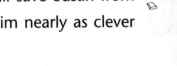

and useful as one of our lesser species and then we can take him home to be our slave – which will be great for us and even better for him of course.

Meanwhile, Bert and Papa were still muttering darkly upstairs. I crept up and put my ear trumpet – switched to full volume – to the door. Papa was going on about getting enough specimens before 'They get here.' Who are They?

Then I heard him ask, 'Do you think it really is Them? How could the Secretive Services have made such a big mistake? How bad could it get?'

To which Bert replied, 'As bad as anything since the Big Bang.' Great.

Yours till the end of time, which may be sooner than we think.

Flowk

MISSION EARTH:
DAY SEVEN SATURDAY

Dear Rok,

The big day today. Susan came to tea. I bet you think it went well. Think again, Rok, think again.

It's the 'weekend' on Saturday and Sunday, so there's no school. We spent all morning getting ready for Susan. The cups and saucers in the whirly washing thing – we found out it was for the clothes, not the plates – didn't stick themselves together, but Farteeta found enough things to hold liquids and food for Susan's visit. Mama also looked up what to give Susan in Professor McSquared's *Guide*:

Make Earth children feel welcome with a super spread of cake, sandwiches (try honey, strawberry jam, or cucumbers) and fancy biscuits. Provide ginger beer for a special treat.

Mama opened the door to him. She had put on some stuff called 'make-up', which made her cheeks very red and she had drawn big blue shadows under her eyeballs.

She invited Susan to smell a colourful flowering vegetable she was wearing on her upper clothing, and then when Susan did, she squirted him with water. I think it was something that came out of the box of children's toys she'd ordered with the stuff. Susan looked unhappy at first, then laughed a bit.

'I didn't know your mum worked in the circus,' he whispered to me, rubbing the water out of his eyeballs.

I don't know what a circus is, so I went 'Ha, ha, ha,' and left it at that.

'How do you do, Susan, I'm so pleased to make

your acquaintance. I hope you liked the very hilarious flower joke. What does your father do?' Mama said, folding back the wet floppy bits of her mouth to show her chewing-blades in a scary way. She has not got used to Earthling expressions.

'I dunno, I've never met him,' said Susan, 'but my mum drives a bus.'

I know what buses are – they're big boxes that move lots of Earthlings around because they're too

primitive to be able to skim or zoom to get to places. But to drive one must mean being a pilot. A female pilot?

Mama said what I was thinking. 'No, no,

Mama says our 'living room' is very elegant.

Mummies can't drive anything.'

'Well, my mum can,' insisted Susan.

He looked round our living room and said, 'What a lot of kettles.'

Take note of the charming 'mice' who scamper around all day. Susan didn't seem to like them. Or the flies.

Then he made that snorting noise Earthlings make when they are trying to keep a laugh inside their heads.

So obviously we've got something wrong in the living room*. Why couldn't Mama have paid a little more attention to Earthling habits? To make it worse, Pluke came in at that moment, looking totally disgusting and drooling spit out of his mouth and wagging his 'tail' and going **WERF**.

Susan thought he was great! Can Susan really be a spiffing fellow, or is he just another filthy slobbering Earthling like all the rest? Pluke started licking Susan's face like a lollipop. Yeeaaacchhh! But Susan loved it!

Pluke is behaving more and more like an Earth dog and seemed to enjoy all the attention, almost as if he likes Susan more than me. I will have to

* Earthlings give their rooms these weird names. I don't think there's a dying room.

keep an eye out though – for all I know Susan will murder Pluke and put him in a sandwich.

'Who's a lovely doggy?' said Susan. 'What's your name?'

'Rhubarb,' said Pluke.

'Did he just speak?' Susan said, his eyeballs very round.

'No, that was me answering for him,' I said thinking quickly. I am beginning to get the hang of this Earth skill called 'lying'.

'But you didn't move your mouth,' Susan said, clapping his hands together. 'How clever! You must have worked in the circus too.'

I must find out what this circus thing is.

'So that's why you started school in the middle of term,' Susan went on. 'You've all been on the road in a caravan, touring! How exciting!'

'Sure,' I said.

'Teatime!' shrieked Mama in her mad Earth

voice. 'I hope you'll agree it's a spiffing spread.'

Mama had got the biggest cake she could find – loads of white cakes piled on top of each other, with a little Earth male and female on top.

'Wow! Who's getting married?' Susan asked.

'One lump or two?' asked Mama, waving a bag of sugar at Susan with one hand and balancing a very tiny pink cup on a large blue plate.

'Do you always drink out of eggcups?' said Susan, looking alarmed.

Worried she'd done something wrong, Mama offered Susan an Earth vegetable called a cucumber, which she'd sliced in half and stuffed with bread and honey. Susan said he wasn't very hungry, just as Farteeta skipped in showing all her chewing-blades and twiddling her stupid yellow hairstyle.

'Hello, Susan,' shouted Farteeta.

'Oh, your little sister's so *cute*,' said Susan. 'I wish I had a little sister.'

'You're a kind boy,' simpered Farteeta. 'Not like Nigel. Papa's got a big surprise for you in the garden.'

Susan looked out the window at the sign Papa had put up.

'Ice cream, that's more like it,' he said, moving towards the door.

'Yes!' squealed Farteeta, bouncing about and waving her horrid fat little Earthling arms. 'The Improver! Susan's going in the Improver!'

As Farteeta bounced, two suckers shot out of her sleeve and her loathsome pink Earthling face started to dissolve, revealing lovely shiny green and violet scales. She was obviously very excited.

Susan shrieked like a *fluit* in a vapouriser.

I poured a whole bottle of *Vom* down Farteeta's throat. She sizzled and turned straight back into Sultana.

'I told you not to play with my circus disguises. Look how you've frightened Susan,' I said quickly. I turned to Susan, saying, 'Typical little sister, eh?'

But all Susan said was, 'W-w-where's the bathroom?'

'Upstairs. Why?'

'I need to go,' and Susan ran upstairs.

Next thing we heard was an ear-trumpet-splitting scream. It was Susan, of course.

'SOMEONE'S SMASHED YOUR TOILET!'

he shrieked.

'Oh *Klong* Almighty and *******' said Mama.

I was shocked. Mama never usually swears that badly.

'Oh yes,' she said. 'I'm so sorry, the doctor's coming to fix it. It'll be ready by, er, by Nigel's birthday party next week.'

'Next *week*?' squealed Susan.

'I mean tonight. Of course. The doctor's coming tonight. He's a top toilet surgeon.'

'But I need to go *now*,' said Susan, crossing his legs weirdly. He pressed some buttons on his mobile (these are the devices Earthlings use to contact each other if they are not in the same room. The poor things don't have any telepathy at all). Minutes later, a huge red beast panted and hooted outside our door. Susan jumped in its mouth without even saying goodbye. How rude.

'You will come to Nigel's party, won't you? Next Thursday? Free ice cream! For the whole class!' shouted Mama desperately as the monster snorted off down the street.

It wasn't a real monster, of course – it was a bus.

Buses don't usually stop in little streets of houses like ours, so Earthlings came out to point and stare. Mr Snell said it was typical of us – we were the neighbours from hell.

Papa shouted from the garden that the Improver was all ready to go.

Mama explained that my friend had left. And why.

Papa shouted at Mama saying the house was *her* business and she should have realised that Earthlings need toilets every day.

Every day. Another horrid piece of news.

'And now Susan will never want to come to tea again!' I said.

'Susan?' said Papa. '*Susan?* But that's a female name! What the *Klagoon* is going on? Surely you know that females are simply un-Improvable?! Their brains are not like ours, you know. Look at your mother and Farteeta.'

'Hmmm, I thought it was a girl, because of the ribbons,' said Farteeta, who's been reading Papa's history books now she's not at playgroup. Then she muttered under her breath, 'Earthling girls have a lot more freedom than I do.'

'I'm beginning to think Earthlings are more advanced than us in some ways,' said Mama, whirling out of the room and slamming the door. Farteeta followed, sticking out her Earth tongue.

What on Faa's got into them?

Papa just sighed. 'What can you do?' And together we checked the interplanet. More bad news: we discovered that nearly all schools on this *Klong*-forsaken planet of gloom allow females to sit alongside males. Well, how was I to tell? They all look the same to me – hideous.

No wonder the place is such a mess. *And* there is no king any more. They have a female king here, called a 'queen'. Obviously Papa hadn't read his history too well – he found this all so upsetting he had to have several spoons of *Koma*, after which he hooked his feet round the lamp fitting and fell fast asleep upside down, just like we do at home.

Now, thanks to Mama stupidly shouting to Susan about my 'birthday'[*], I will have to have my whole class over to a party, all doing poo-poos and wee-wees in our house. *And* I have wasted a week making friends with a girl.

And, *squilloons*! I forgot to memory-blast Susan! Now she will tell my whole class about the suckers and the circus and the no-toilet situation.

Life isn't worth living.

Your sad friend,
   Flowk

* Birthdays. You get presents every single year just for being alive.

MISSION EARTH: DAY EIGHT SUNDAY

Hi Rok,

No school today either, so as the single sun was shining for the first time since we arrived we ventured out as a family to see how Earthlings spend their free time. Papa warned us yet again to avoid cars – ruthless machines which slaughter 1.2 million Earthlings every year. We all took a dose of *Vom*, in case anything too exciting happened, and Papa insisted we all had Faa air cylinders in case the fumes overcame us. I don't know how he thinks I survive at school every day.

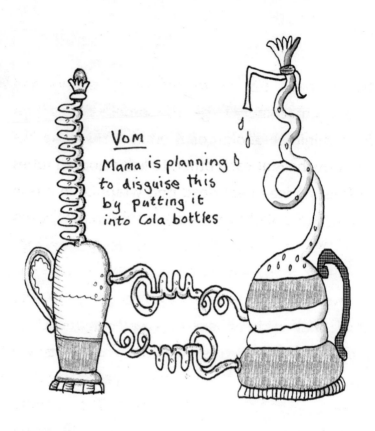

VOM

Mama is planning
to disguise this
by putting it
into Cola bottles

Finally we made it round the corner to the local 'park' (which, by the way, Papa had checked out to make sure was free of spinach). It's like a big football pitch but oddly decorated with dog poo-poos and little plastic bottles and bags. Earthlings try to have fun using swinging, sliding and rotating machinery to get the same feeling we do from minimal looping or zooming. They also like to throw balls at each other, to lick coloured tubes of freezing ice or eat dead dog wrapped in a bun (these are called 'hot dogs'. I suckered Pluke in case they decided to use him). For swimming, they have a tiny outside 'pool' of water just a few metres deep, in which they flap sadly up and down. Half of them have to have flotation aids to avoid drowning as they have no gills. If they are not in parks, Papa says, they are glued (this means, literally, stuck) to their TVs, or the internet, which is like the interplanet only slower by a factor of eight billion. Sometimes they visit supply zones called 'shops', or big TVs called 'cinemas'. They are happy, Rok, in their simple way.

Papa made us all go home after about five

minutes of this. He said the poo-poos would give us germs.

Mama was in an odd mood and kept making strange remarks. 'There's a mummy driving,' or, 'Look, there's a female in a police uniform,' or 'See? Papas *do* carry babies!'

'Nonsense,' said Papa. 'You can't possibly tell the genders apart. You're giving Farteeta ideas.'

'I think Farteeta's got ideas already,' snapped Mama. 'Let's go to the cinema.'

'Absolutely not. Think of the radiation!'

I don't know who is more peculiar at the moment, Mama or Papa.

Back home, Bert had locked himself upstairs, fuming and buzzing and saying he can't defend us from the approaching Thing all on his own. Papa looked panicky and rushed up to help him. I followed and banged on the door. Papa opened it, but wouldn't let me in.

'UNDERAGE. UNSUITABLE CONTENT,' said Bert.

'Go away, this is something I hope you'll never have to see,' said Papa, his voice shaking. 'Bert and I will sort it out, don't worry,' he added, but his Earth face was looking very worried indeed. I didn't budge. I could hear Bert fizzing and fuming in the background, but I couldn't make out what he was saying.

'Papa, please tell me what this Thing that's coming is. I want to be brave and true and get Space Explorer Level One.'

'You'd get Level Ten if you could handle this, but you can't. Stick to your own mission. You've got to find a boy to test the Improver. The Emperor needs only the best.'

'But how can I tell boys from girls?'

'Boys wear trousers,' said Papa, looking exasperated. I told him that nearly everyone wears trousers. I was playing for time, trying to make sense of Bert's zinging and bleeping.

'Run all your class's first names through the interplanet. That should tell you.'

'But maybe none of the boys in my class will want to come back to Faa,' I said, straining my ear trumpets to hear Bert.

'Want? *Want?* What does it matter what they want? You're not getting funny ideas too, are you? Earthlings are, in fact, under a great threat. We're not sure what it is, but it could destroy Earth. And unless we save a few, they'll all die!'

At this, Bert set up such a commotion that Papa was forced to close the door.

So that's why we're really here, I think. Papa has been sent to save Earth from a deadly threat. If so, why didn't he tell us before?

Your confused friend,
Flowk

Dearest Rok,

I slept even worse than usual. Bert and Papa were up all night again.

'Remember only to invite someone home with a boy's name,' said Papa, as I left for school. 'But be sure to ask them if they're a boy too, just to be on the safe side.'

So today I examined everyone very carefully, based on my interplanet name checks. I didn't tell Papa I'd found out that 'Miss' means female, so Miss Barn, and even our headteacher, are both female! That means Earthlings allow females to do everything! It's also weird to think that Carmel and Jatinder and Sophie, who are all in the top group, Moles, are *girls*. But I'm beginning to think Mama's right, and that males and females aren't that different. Funny to think that Earthlings, who are so dim in so many ways, have discovered this before we have. Don't laugh at me, Rok. If you think hard about it, you might agree. Your great-great granny was a pilot, wasn't she, before the Emperor vapourised her for disobedience? (Sorry to bring up old wounds, but I think we may have been wrong about one or two things. Please delete this passage if you're putting it on your blog, by the way. I don't want the Secretive Services thinking I am disloyal.) But back to my mission.

Susan didn't sit next to me. At lunchtime she was pointing at me and making that nice, giggly sound.

Why on Faa do Earthlings eat their pets when they could have chocolate all day?

To see my Earth face eat
the chocolate, move the
page slowly towards you
until your beak touches
the planet.

Roddy's mum brought him to tea later on.
'The toilet surgeon's been! It's working!'

shrieked Mama brightly, offering her a plate of mushrooms with Marmite.

Roddy's mum said sorry, but you either love it or you hate it, then flapped around telling Roddy to remember his manners. She seemed to want to stay for longer, but Roddy had spotted *Grand Theft Spacecraft: Invasion*.

'Want to play that!' he shouted.

It was fun. We killed four thousand aliens (who looked strangely like the evil race of Threggs).

But it was more than just fun, Rok. When we destroyed the final alien spacecraft there was an incredible sound, like nothing I've ever heard before. It's a range of differently pitched noises, high, low, medium, some short and soft, some long and explosive, then short loud sounds and long rippling quiet sounds and all of them vibrating in rapid succession. But this description doesn't begin to do it justice, because each of the sounds flows into the next as though the sound itself is looping or zooming! My ear trumpets tingled and my heads spun round and shot out of my vest. Roddy was too involved in the game to notice, but I had to swallow a whole jug of *Vom*.

'What's *that*?' I asked.

'What's what?' said Roddy.

'That amazing sound.'

'Oh, that's the *Grand Theft Spacecraft: Invasion* theme tune,' said Roddy, as if it was nothing special.

'Play it again! I must hear it again!'

'Ice cream time!' shouted Mama. 'Come on! It's in the garden shed!' And before I could alert Papa, Roddy hurtled outside straight into the Improver!

'Wait!' shouted Papa, racing after him, clutching the Improver's remote. '*Klong* knows what will happen!'

We stood staring at the open shed door.

Roddy had vanished.

'Why did you let him go in before I'd started it up?' shouted Papa.

'How was I to know he'd run off like that?' said Mama. 'Can't you start it now?'

'We don't know where he is. He could be in the exercise tunnel, or the polishing tube, or anywhere. If he's in the wrong place at the wrong time, the blades could chop off his head, or the calculator's circuits could fry his brain. It all needs to be carefully synchronised on entry, you know. Fine-tuned, to the height and weight of the individual Earthling,' said Papa, rapidly pushing some buttons on the Improver's controls. 'Well, perhaps it doesn't matter. There are plenty more. Boys, I mean, not heads.'

But I was getting fond of Roddy, like you feel about a new pet.

'Roddy! Come out!' I shouted, zooming towards

the now buzzing, flashing, vibrating Improver.

Papa suckered me. 'I don't want your heads chopped off too!'

Clouds of blue vapour steamed out of the Improver's funnels. A screeching wail echoed from inside, and a vast green ice cube shot out of the Improver's ejection chute. Inside it was Roddy!

'*Klong* Almighty!' said Papa. 'The cooler system's in overdrive!'

'Quick,' shouted Mama. 'Hot water bottles!'

We filled all sixty-eight hot water bottles to unfreeze Roddy, whose head unfroze first. He looked like a *krakwurzle* stuck in a *pllorq*.

'No free ice cream for Roddy!' he moaned, just as his mum arrived to pick him up. I gave him *Grand Theft Spacecraft: Invasion* to shut him up, while I was hunting for the memory-blaster.

'Don't tell my mum,' he said, stuffing it into his rucksack. 'She might notice it's an eighteen.'

'Did you have a nice time?' asked his mum.

'Lovely,' said Roddy. 'I got frozen in the big machine in the shed.'

'He's such an imaginative boy. I wish people understood him better. Thank you so much for having him Mrs Colander.'

No need to use the memory blaster on Roddy.

'What a hopeless case,' said Papa, when they'd gone. 'Just goes to show there's no point in doing this the kind way. We'll put the Improver on full strength for your birthday party and shove the whole class in, females and all.'

'I thought you said it needed to be fine tuned to the person,' I said.

'If we lose a few, never mind. The Threggs will finish them all off anyway,' Papa replied.

'Threggs?'

'Just a joke,' said Papa quickly, disappearing upstairs to Bert.

He and Bert are getting worse and worse. Bert never comes out of his room. He is either raving or sulking and won't give us news from Faa. Not even the *fatool* scores. As for mentioning Threggs, that is not my idea of a joke.

I have been trying to remember the theme tune on *Grand Theft Spacecraft: Invasion*. I wish I hadn't let Roddy have it. I can't stop thinking about those amazing sounds. They gave me feelings I have never had before.

Please send me the *fatool* scores!

Your friend,
Flowk

P.S. I bet you think I might have needed the toilet after that chocolate, but no, it was OK. We Faathings can digest anything. I'm going to bring some back with me. I've checked it out. It is good for you, with lots of iron. So is spinach, come to that. But Papa isn't afraid of chocolate.

Roddy gave me all these Earth 'sweeties'. The shiny 'wrappers' are nice and crunchy.

MISSION EARTH: DAY TEN TUESDAY

Dear Rok,

Amazing scores! I can't believe those *fnurfling* Pyez from Asteroid 97 are in the Intergalactic league – last time I saw them play they lost fifty of their team in a black hole and another ten looped straight into a meteor shower, losing a record two billion games in a row. But listen, I've discovered something even more exciting than *fatool*.

The theme tune is explained!

I have heard more of these extraordinary new sounds. They are the first really not-ugly noises on

this horrid planet, Rok! How I wish I could describe them to you! We did them at school today. The individual sounds are called 'notes' and when blended together, they are called 'music'.

This is what happened. First, Miss Barn let us listen to some music. All of it flowed out of a tiny silver disc! I turned my ear trumpets to top volume for only the second time since I've been on Earth.

It made me feel like flying, looping, zooming, eating chocolate and playing *fatool* all at the same time.

Roddy and Susan even made some extra bits of it on music furniture.

Miss Barn says they are 'gifted and talented'. This usually means someone who can read a whole book or do very simple equations, but for once I agreed with her.

Susan then did a small 'song' which is talking with the music. I was so excited I had to swig some *Vom*, but I couldn't help trying to join in.

You know the noise you make when one head is gargling in plasma and another gets hiccups? That was me.

Everyone laughed.

'Be quiet! We never laugh *at* each other, only *with* each other,' said Miss Barn, which shows she knows less than a *fluit*.

So I just listened, and as I was listening my hearts seemed to expand inside me and my eyeballs overflowed with liquid, just as if I was crying like a weedy Earthling.

Carmel gave me a tissue, a flimsy thing they use for their bogies. No thanks!

At lunchtime, I felt as emotional as a herd of *muffoons*. I was thinking so hard about the music that I didn't see Colin Snell lurking by the room where they all go for poo-poos. He pulled me in and – horrible to relate – tried to push my head inside a toilet.

'My dad's going to kill your rubbish dog! Fi Fi

might get mongrel puppies.'

I was so disgusted, I nearly forgot myself and vapourised him, but I collected my wits just in time to unfurl three minimal extenders and flip him head first into the toilet. It was either him or me, Rok. It wasn't my fault that whoever had been in there before hadn't flushed it.

Back 'home' (I only really think of Faa, not our Earth house, when I use this word), Mama and Farteeta were unpacking enormous boxes while Papa was making frantic adjustments to the Improver and Bert was steaming and whistling and mumbling, 'Spinach! Threggs! Traversing the large Magellenic cloud. Passing the Andromeda Galaxy!' What does it all mean, Rok? I fear for our sanity in this grisly dump.

'Just in time – you can help us unpack,' said Mama when she saw me. *Klong!* All I wanted to do

was go to my room to think about music.

Mama had ordered more 'toys', because Farteeta has been nagging her: 'dolls' (miniature Earthlings made of plastic, with scary blue eyeballs like Colin Snell), 'teddies' (bizarre pretend pets), badly constructed miniature vehicles, science kits for doing experiments just like our scientists did a billion centuries ago. And *Klagoon*! A music machine just like the one Miss Barn had put the silver discs in at school. I suckered it.

'I told you, you are not to use those machines!' screeched Papa, zooming in from the garden and snatching it away. 'They are just there to make us look like Earthlings. They might be very dangerous to us.'

'But the sounds this makes are magic,' I said. 'They're called music.'

'Never heard of it,' said Papa. 'If it's anything like these books and pictures it will just fill your head with nonsense. The sooner we can Improve your classmates and get away from here the better.'

'But suppose the Improver goes wrong?' I said. 'Suppose it hurts them?'

'Don't be ridiculous. I've told you, they have no feelings to speak of!'

'But they might *die*. I thought you wanted to *save* them. I thought we were goodies!'

'Of course we're goodies, but you can't save every member of every single species in the Universe, you know that. Anyway, time is short.'

Papa beckoned me into the kitchen. 'I don't want Farteeta and Mama to hear about this, but as you already know, Bert has been picking up some very disturbing signals from hyperspace. They sound like —'

'MONSTERS! AAAAAAAARGH!'

came a scream from Colin Snell's garden next door.

'They can't have got here already, surely?' said Papa, panicking.

'Call the vet!' Mr Snell shouted.

'They're monsters! Poor Fi Fi!' said Colin.

Papa and me raced outside and looked over the fence. Mama and Farteeta were already there.

Fi Fi was lying on the grass with five babies dancing around her! She looked very happy, which is more than you could say about Colin Snell and his parents.

See? They are half Pluke and half Fi Fi. We have

created a new race!

'Now we'll be in trouble,' said Papa, ducking out of sight.

'No, we won't,' said Farteeta. 'Earth puppies take two whole months to grow, whereas Faa pets take only two days. The Snells will never think it's our fault.'

Female brains really aren't that bad. Farteeta knows more stuff about Earth than Papa . . .

Papa disappeared upstairs as usual with Bert, taking the music machine with him. It didn't have any of the little silver discs with it anyway, so I guess it wouldn't have worked. But Papa's behaviour's so frustrating. I'm going to find out more about these hyperspace signals tomorrow, even if I have to break Bert's door down. Something very dangerous is going on, Rok. Very.

Flowk

Maybe goodies and baddies are not so different after all, Rok. Does this say 'GOOD' or 'EVIL'?
———>

MISSION EARTH: DAY ELEVEN WEDNESDAY

Hey Rok,

What a day. First thing, I tried to batter down Bert's door. It should have been easy, being made of flimsy tree vegetable matter, but of course, Bert had reinforced it with tungsten, titanium, tantalum and vanadium embedded in a matrix of cobalt. I should have known. Papa shouted at me from inside but I didn't stop until I'd made him promise to reveal all to me after school.

Next thing, Mr Snell came round clasping a bunch of thorny vegetables.

'I've come to apologise. Fi Fi's puppies are obviously nothing to do with your Rupert. They look a little like her but nothing at all like him. And she's only known him a few days. I'm so sorry if you thought us rude. I hope these roses will make up for it . . .'

'Not at all,' said Mama, recoiling from the vegetables and flashing her terrifying smile. 'Do come in and have a bottle of whisky.'

'That'll go very well with my cornflakes,' said Mr Snell, backing away and bumping into Pluke, who jumped up. He was begging to be let out to see his puppies, although luckily Mr Snell couldn't understand a word he said. Pluke's only allowed to say 'Werf' ever since the incident with Susan.

'But they are my children! They've all got two heads just like my third daddy,' said Pluke after Mr Snell had gone. 'They are in the hands of the Enemy!'

I comforted him, saying we'd sort out a visit to Fi Fi.

'The sooner we can Improve your classmates the better,' hissed Mama. 'That was a narrow escape.'

At school, everyone was talking about the monster pups from outer space, who'd already got their picture in the newspaper.

Colin Snell said his dad had been paid lots of money and that the puppies were going to be on TV. 'Wasn't your dog though, so you don't get any money,' he said to me, but he was smiling. I think the head-in-toilet moment has made him want to be my friend. I'll never understand Earthlings.

After lunch, Miss Barn told us about a thing called 'global warming' where Earth is over-heating. Papa had mentioned it, but I had no idea how bad it was. I then recalled it had happened on Faa in the Fourth Quadratic period but our genius scientists cured it by shooting sulphate into the sky to make a sunscreen, whereas Earthlings, who only have one measly sun, don't seem to worry about it that much, even though they know it's happening. They drive cars to school even when it is a few minutes to walk. I suppose it is because they can't zoom and because everything here is so ugly they don't like walking about and having to look at it all.

'You're right, Earth is doomed,' I said to Papa when I got home.

'How do you know that?' said Papa. 'I only just discovered it.'

'We learned all about it today. Global warming.'

'Oh, *that*,' said Papa. 'I thought you meant the invasion.'

'Invasion?'

'I was about to tell you last night, when Pluke's fatherhood event stopped me. It's really bad, Flowkwee. Catastrophic in fact. But I promised to tell you, so I will. I want you to be brave and true and listen carefully.'

At last, Papa was talking to me like a grown-up. I stood ready to do my duty, my ear trumpets tuned, my courage high.

'It's an invasion force, I'm afraid,' Papa said. 'It will wipe out Earth and everything on it. It's Threggs.'

Threggs! A true Faathing knows no fear. But I shivered in all my suckers.

'But Papa, the Emperor can stop them, surely? If not, he would never have sent us here. He never sends his loyal subjects to their doom.' A disloyal thought occurred to me then. 'Or does the Emperor know?'

'Apparently the Emperor has known about it for some time,' Papa said, his Earth face turning pink, 'which was why he wanted us to get specimens to take home, before Earthlings become extinct. But he didn't want to alarm us.'

'What do you mean, he didn't want to alarm us? We could be killed!' I shouted.

'Don't you dare question the Emperor's decisions!' said Papa. 'Remember, you are a Faathing brave and true, and what the Emperor says, goes. The Secretive Services made a few minor space/time calculations, thinking we would get here in 1942, do

some good by stopping the World War and still have plenty of time to make a few trips back and forth to bring Earth specimens home. We had to Improve them first, of course, otherwise they'd be useless to us. The Secretive Services calculated the Threggs would take about sixty-five Earth years to arrive, because their galaxy is a few billion light years away. It's just that we arrived here at roughly the same time as them. It's an easy mistake to make.'

Easy mistake? I could tell Papa didn't really think so. He looked stricken.

'Listen, Flowkwee,' he said. 'I haven't got much respect for Earthlings, but I did feel if we could Improve them, they might have a better life.'

I can't believe our noble Secretive Services could be so dumb, Rok, but I felt sorry for Papa, so I tried to look on the bright side.

'We defeated the Threggs back at the dawn of time, didn't we? So we'll defeat them again,' I said.

'We repelled them,' said Papa. 'But we didn't exterminate them.'

'But what could they possibly want on Earth?'

'Hah! Bert's found that out at last. They want to colonise Earth because of the spinach here.'

'So that's why you've been frightened of spinach,' I said.

'I have not been frightened of spinach! I have been concerned about its power to attract Threggs! It's like a magnet to them. They must have magnesium, iron, and vitamin K otherwise their brains, such as they are, implode. They are stupid creatures and have never got used to the fact that even when you have an enormous bunch of spinach it reduces to an eighth of its size when it's cooked. They can never, ever get enough. They've invaded billions of planets and searched galaxies in all thirteen dimensions and now they're headed here. They'll vapourise every living thing except the

spinach plant. Then they'll grow it all over Earth.'
Papa put his Earth head in his hands and I could see
his dear old unhappy face peeping out of his jacket.
I patted his back and gave him a sip of *Vom*.

'Are you quite certain Threggs digest the same
food as Earthlings?' I asked.

'Most singular brained creatures in primitive eco-
systems eat the same food, you should know that.'

Maybe we can eat the same food too, I thought,
remembering my chocolate experience. But I didn't
tell Papa. I didn't want to make him feel more foolish
than he was feeling already.

'And if they invade, Earth will be a spinach
garden? Without any people? Or computer games?
Or music? Threggs will destroy everything?'

'Correct. As you know, back in the Sixth Quadratic
Wars, Threggs vapourised half the population of Faa
in their quest for spinach, which doesn't even grow
on Faa! They're not fussy who they vapourise. But

finally our generals foiled them.'

'How?'

'That's the big problem. Bert still can't work it out. Back then, computers had such simple memory chips that Bert's enormous brain can't slow down enough to untangle all the data. It *appears* we knew something then that we've forgotten since. It's like searching for a needle in a camel. (*Editor's note: Translator, please check this.*) It's unlikely we'll work it out before Flyzoop arrives to take us home.'

'Flyzoop?'

'I told you, he's on standby. I know he's a fool, and a hopeless pilot, but he's the only Faathing within a billion light years. I booked him for eight o'clock tomorrow evening, after your party. By then we'll have shoved your class through the Improver so we can take the survivors back to Faa.'

'You mean we're just abandoning Earth and everything on it?'

'Obviously. Do you want to stay and be obliterated by Threggs? They don't do it nicely, you know. It hurts.'

So there you have it, Rok. Threggs. They gave me nightmares when I was little and they still do.

But suddenly I'm worried about leaving Earth.

Will we be allowed to bring Fi Fi and her puppies? Supposing Susan doesn't get Improved? Or Roddy? Will they be left to the Threggs? What will happen to Miss Barn? I was even enjoying the story she read to us this week. Now I'll never know how it ended. I've realised made up stories can be exciting. And computer games, too. And chocolate. And, I admit it, even girls aren't so bad. But the best thing about Earth is the music.

I have changed, Rok, I have changed. If you don't hear from me again, I leave you my *fatool* boots.

Tomorrow's *the* day. My 'birthday'. The Improver. Threggs.

You can have my *flonkblatter* collection, too.

Yours in the abyss of a deep gravitational well,

Flowk

MISSION EARTH:
DAY TWELVE THURSDAY

My 'birthday'

Rok,

I'm sending this in infernal conditions. I know it only takes me a nano-second to write thirty thousand words, but even so I might be vapourised any moment. I'll start at the beginning and hope I get to the end before the End gets to me.

All day long, people kept asking me what I'd got for my birthday. I thought fast and said some toy vehicles and a teddy. They did the *plongule* laughing again.

Susan has been telling the entire class that my family are all in the circus, so they were expecting us to eat fire and do simple gravity-calculations called 'juggling'. Farteeta has been practising.

Sure enough, Mama opened the door with her red cheeks and blue eyeballs on and a huge red smile, and Farteeta stood behind her, juggling all sixty-eight kettles, so that was a success. But underneath Mama's big red smile I could see her unhappy face was working hard not to be noticed. Maybe Papa had told her about the Threggs?

'Don't let anyone into the kitchen,' she hissed.

But it is hard to keep twenty-eight Earthlings in order, as Miss Barn is always pointing out. They all ran into the house yelling, 'Where's the tight-rope?' and six of them headed for the kitchen.

Papa was hanging upside down from the ceiling light, fast asleep. Farteeta was hanging from his arms trying to wake him up.

'Here's Nigel's dad – he's an acrobat,' they all shouted. Maybe that's a bat who isn't mad.

'Whoa, cola, wicked,' said Aaron Ratchet. I knew Mama shouldn't have put the *Vom* in a 'cola' bottle for disguise, but I couldn't stop him taking a swig, because Farteeta was gesturing dementedly in my direction.

She pulled me aside. 'I know everything. I've been working with Bert for two days,' she whispered. 'Papa's drunk too much *Koma*, but Bert's been blowing his circuits all day. He's finally got the names of some of the instrument panel that created the Thregg-mashing sound waves back in the Sixth Quadratic Wars. As well as mashing the Thregg army they created fourteen new quasars, six thousand languages, twenty-eight new religions and provided eighteen thousand galaxies with hot and cold running water and free cinema tickets on Wednesdays. So they must have outstanding megalocity.'

I couldn't believe it! My annoying sister is the one who's really been in charge of stuff back here while I've been at school learning zero.

'So what are these instruments called? And what do they look like?'

'Well, in English, Bert thinks they're called peeanners, strumpets, vilins, harpies and floooots. But we've no idea what they look like.'

Peeanners and floooots. I knew I'd heard something like that before. But where?

'We have to see Bert,' I said, heading upstairs.

'Oh no you don't,' said Mama, suckering me with her centrifugal extender. 'You're not leaving me alone with this lot of *krooligans*.'

My class were throwing thousands of cushions. Maybe most Earth houses don't have so many.

'TEATIME!' shouted Mama. 'I'll give you each one hundred pounds if you're good.'

'Nah. You're winding us up,' said Jatinder.

Mama waved a lot of money papers and everyone went very polite.

Everybody got a loaf of bread with some lovely looking green spheres called brussel sprouts stuffed inside. Mama had made a giant roast potato-flavoured jelly, too. I was proud of her. It was a shame no one seemed hungry.

'Time for your circus ride,' said Papa, his Earth eyeballs red and bleary from his nap, as he lurched outside to open the shed door.

The Improver whirred and rattled and glowed a shimmering silver-turning-pink colour, as if it was heating up.

'I'm not going in that,' Colin Snell said.

'Nor me,' said Jatinder.

Even Susan looked doubtful.

'Have you tried it yourself?' she asked me. 'Are you sure it's safe?'

Pluke!
Eeeek!

FREE
ICE
CREAM!
Any flavour you like plus
fudge sauce and choc flake!

'Look, the doggy's doing it!' Roddy said.

Oh, no! I looked round, and saw Pluke's tail disappearing into the Improver.

'Rhubarb!' I shouted. 'Don't go in there!'

'Why not?' asked Aaron Ratchet. 'You said it was fine for us to.'

It was too late. Pluke disappeared inside the Improver and I heard its engines start up.

I watched in horror. Everybody else stood around scratching themselves and picking their beaks. But not when Pluke shot out the other end at three times his usual size, although luckily still disguised as a dog (we'd all taken extra *Vom* this morning, in case the party got too exciting). Obviously, the Improver's able to do all sorts of stuff Papa never dreamed of including Improving Earth bodies to Faa dimensions.

First Pluke walked on his back legs. Then he turned a somersault. Then he pounced on Aaron Ratchet's football, spun it up into the air with one foot, balanced it on his beak, flipped over on to his front feet and balanced it on his back ones. Then he headed it over the garden fence. Everybody clapped wildly.

'Fetch the ball, Superdoggy!' shouted Aaron Ratchet. Pluke leaped into the air and somersaulted over the fence. There was a lot of crashing about, then the ball came flying back over the fence, followed by Pluke, with Fi Fi on his back.

'Oh no,' I said to myself as Pluke and Fi Fi hurtled towards the entrance to the Improver. I shot out a sucker to catch Pluke's back legs but he was too quick for me. The Improver whirred and shook and glowed again and out came Pluke and a gigantic Fi Fi. This time they ran all down the garden heading the ball to each other.

'Barcelona couldn't do that,' said Adam Three.

'Awesome,' said Aaron Ratchet, who, after finishing the bottle of *Vom*, had turned from a fat Earthling into a thin one. Is being spherical some kind of Earthling disguise, cured by *Vom*?

'Does this machine work with everything?' asked Adam One, grabbing a toy batmobile from Farteeta's new toybox and hurling it into the Improver. After some shaking and rattling, the batmobile squeezed out of the other end like Earth chewing-blade paste from a tube, then swelled up into a big black quivering, smoking machine half the length of Susan's mother's bus.

'Wicked,' said Orville Muffin.

Colin Snell managed to scramble out of the way just in time, as Aaron, Orville, Annie Spratt and Adams One and Three jumped into the batmobile and set its jet engines roaring. It crashed through the Snells' fence, flattened a lot of the vegetables, a stone fountain, and a table and chairs, skidded round in a circle and shot back through the fence before its yelling drivers brought it to a halt.

Mr Snell came rushing after the batmobile, red and shouting. But he stopped, his mouth flapping up and down and no sound coming out, when an Earth creature I'd never seen before – wearing almost no tubes and flaps and with a very long shiny yellow hairstyle – squirmed out of the Improver and stood in front of him, wiggling its middle bits and showing all its gleaming chewing-blades.

'Hi, honey,' it said. 'Want to play with me?'

Mr Snell went white and fell to the ground, gasping.

'What on Faa's that?' I said to Farteeta.

'It's something called a Barby doll,' Farteeta said, clapping her hands and laughing. 'It was one of the Earth toys Mama got me. Much Improved, isn't it?'

'This is the best circus I've ever been to,' said Aaron Ratchet, shaking hands with me like a grown-up. 'It's a privilege to be your manager.'

Papa took one look at the Barby-person and fell down alongside Colin's dad. How feeble.

I could hear Mama screaming, and turned to see her running out of the house, following Sophie and Jatinder, who were carrying our TV. Into the Improver it went. Aaron Ratchet and Orville Muffin started turning the dials and flipping the switches on the Improver's controls.

The TV bubbled, smoked and squeezed out of

the exit. It looked much the same.

'It doesn't just Improve things by making them bigger you know,' said Farteeta. 'It made the toy car's engine work. It can do almost anything, if you know how.' She winked at me and plugged the TV into the Improver's circuits. Immediately the screen lit up and the TV rumbled, shivered and let out whistling deep-space noises.

A blurred picture formed. Everybody stopped to watch, transfixed. They could tell this was no ordinary TV programme because a repulsive purple oily face filled the screen. In *four* dimensions.

'GREETINGS, EARTHLINGS,'

it roared, swivelling six crusty yellow eyeballs and showing a mouthful of chewing-blades curved and thin-tipped like knives.

Threggs. Living, breathing Threggs. That haven't been seen since the Sixth Quadratic Wars . . .

'We were beginning to think you'd never tune in,' the evil voice continued. 'We'll be relaying this message to your whole pathetic race, soon, before we annihilate everything else on your putrid planet. Everything except for your beautiful spinach.'

Everybody screamed. Farteeta, Mama and me just stared in horror. If we hadn't taken a triple dose of *Vom* in preparation for the party, our disguises would have betrayed us there and then.

'Let me introduce myself,' said the oily purple monstrosity. 'I am Keith, King of Threggs, Lord of the Loonyverse, Destroyer of Souls, Spinach Finder General. We do hope you're enjoying your party,' the slavering purple face went on, looking out around the garden. 'Just as well, since it'll be your *last*. We'll be there before the next setting of your worthless Sun. And then you'll never have to see it rise again. Won't that be a relief?

'Ha ha ha! HA HA HA HA HA. HO HEE HOOO HA HA HA HA HA! SO VERY SORRY! HOO HOO HOO!'

'**WANT TO GO HOME,**' wailed all the class except Roddy, Susan – and Colin Snell. Mr Snell, who was just shaking his head and getting up after seeing the Barby, went even whiter and fell over asleep again. Papa was out cold. Mama had

Keith, King of Threggs. In a good mood.

zoomed inside in search of *Vom*, thinking our triple dose would not be strong enough and hoping to protect us for a little longer. It was up to us younglings to save the day.

'Memory-blast your friends and send them home, quick,' Farteeta hissed at me. 'And let's get off this doomed planet before those . . . those . . . Things . . . get here. The mission's over. We tried.'

Everyone was running towards the house. I pulled the memory-blaster out of my pocket and zapped the yelling, stampeding group. They all stopped running and clustered around Mama, who had come downstairs unable to find any *Vom*, but who was now handing out fistfuls of Earth money and flashing her chewing-blades, looking almost as scary as a Thregg.

'Party bags! Party bags!' everyone shouted. 'Happy birthday, Nigel!' The memory-blaster had obviously worked.

Mama shot a relieved look at Farteeta and me

and led them inside the house to get their coats. Mama was being brave and true by sending them all home happy, you'll agree, but she hadn't noticed that Roddy, Susan and Colin had stayed behind watching the TV screen. By now, other purple monstrous faces were gathering around the first one, laughing louder and louder.

'Hi, you guys,' the Barby said to them. 'Coming to the beach with me? We can dance and have a little fun.'

She turned on the pink radio she was carrying and a strange and clangy, but quite tuneful, Earth music came out of it. Farteeta's mouth opened and her eyes stretched wide.

'How beautiful,' she said, swaying and waving her arms about.

The purple monsters stopped laughing. They covered their scaly ears and let out horrible ghostly groans. Suddenly the signal was cut and the TV screen went dark. We could still hear the muffled voice of Keith, King of the Threggs. 'Don't worry, feeble Earthlings. We'll be arriving shortly,' he was saying. 'Or rather DO worry. Worry very much indeed. Be very, very worried.

'HAR HAR HAR. HOO.'

The Barby pouted and turned her radio off. Farteeta grabbed it and tried to turn it back on, but it just spouted an Earth weather forecast.

I pointed the memory-blaster at Roddy and Susan and Colin.

'Zap them,' said Farteeta.

'Wait,' said Susan. And I did. 'You just changed my friends with that, didn't you?' Susan said, pointing to the memory-blaster. 'You made them forget all this. You're not human, are you?'

'No,' I said. 'I'm not.'

'Zap her!' said Farteeta, trying to wrestle the memory-blaster from me.

'When you painted my picture,' Susan was saying, 'with that funny arm you pretend you haven't got, the way you play football . . . I knew it!'

'Sorry,' I said.

'You brought those Things here to kill us all, didn't you?' Susan said, looking very fierce and beginning to shake me by the arms. 'To kill the class, and me, and my mum and granny and cat and budgie and *everything*.'

'NO, I DIDN'T,' I shouted at her. 'I didn't know anything about them till now. We just came here to help. We came to Improve you all.'

'We don't want Improving, thank you,' Susan said, letting me go and turning away with a sad look. 'We're fine as we are.'

We all stood around for a while, not knowing

what to do. 'Don't look so sad,' the Barby said to us. 'Let's all go shopping.'

'OH SHUT UP,' we all shouted at her.

She pouted again. 'I'll just wear my happy face until y'all feel better,' she said.

'I've got an idea,' said Farteeta, fiddling with the controls of the Improver. A loud sucking noise came from the exit tube, the Barby squealed as she disappeared into it, and in a flash popped out the front end as a doll again.

Hey. Look at Barby's face when she goes back in the Improver. Turn it upside down to see what I mean.

'Shame we can't do that with those monsters,' said Colin Snell.

'Can't anything stop them?' Susan asked.

'Not now,' I said. 'Our only hope is to get off Earth before they get any nearer. Maybe we can take you with us. You'll have a nice life on Faa – it's a wonderful place. We won't make you work too hard, and think how useful you'll be in our experiments. You'll be able to teach us so much about primitive life forms.'

'Primitive?! And what about everybody else, everybody you don't take with you?' Susan asked, as if she couldn't believe what I'd said. 'We're just an experiment to you, that's all. What about our families, and their families and everybody's families? And all the animals and plants and oceans and mountains and clouds and trees . . . and . . . and . . .'

'There's probably more of them in the Universe somewhere, if you're that keen on them,' Farteeta shrugged. 'It's infinite, you know.'

'They didn't like the Barby doll's music, did they?' squeaked Roddy, in a tiny voice.

'Who would?' snorted Colin Snell. 'That song was even cheesy when my dad was my age.'

'No, wait,' Susan said. 'He's right – they didn't like it. You could see they didn't. They made horrible unhappy noises and covered their nasty scaly ears.'

'There's nothing wrong with scales,' I said to her. If she's going to live on Faa, it's right she should know these things.

'They . . . didn't . . . like . . . the . . . music,' Roddy repeated.

'Yes, I know,' snapped Farteeta. 'That's why I kept this, but it won't make any more sounds.' She threw the Barby radio on the ground.

'Wait, that's given me an idea . . . Roddy!' I shouted. 'What was the music furniture called that you played on?'

'Piano.'

'Peeanner! And what did you play, Susan?'

'Flute.'

'Floooot! Of course. Go and get them. Quick!'

'My flute's in my bag,' said Susan, and she ran off into the house for it.

'I'm not Superman, though,' Roddy complained. 'I can't carry a big piano all the way from my house, especially not running.'

'You won't need to!' shouted Farteeta. 'There's a little thing in the toy box that has the word *piano* on it. With a bit of Improving it can be as big as you like.'

'My dad's got a lot of electric stuff he uses for deejaying down the pub,' said Colin Snell. 'You know, drums, guitar. I'll see what I can find.'

Farteeta looked up, excited. 'Guitar! Yes! Of course, I read about that on the internet. Get that!'

I found out later why she was so excited, but as

Colin rushed off she got the toy piano, put it in the Improver and pressed the buttons. She's really mastered the Improver's controls. Pretty soon, a kind of shiny black and white jelly and a tangle of wires flopped out the other end, shook itself, and stood up as a massive piano with a lid.

'Wow,' sighed Roddy. 'A proper nine-footer.'

Susan came out with her flute and those strange music books with lots of dots written on lots of lines. But she looked as if something unhappy had occurred to her.

'What's the point of this?' she asked. 'Those horrible monsters don't have to listen to us – they can invade Earth just as easily with their sound-systems on mute. It isn't going to work.'

I realised she was right, but a familiar rumbling announced the arrival of Bert! It was such a surprise to see him out there in the garden that I almost fell over. He was bleeping and whirring excitedly, and

carrying a strange machine he must have been
building in his room.

'Threggsfleet!   Threggsfleet!'   he
gibbered electronically. 'Lockedit! Lockedit!
Locked on to the carrier!'

'What do you mean, Bert?' I asked, grabbing him by the upper hinges.

Bert was so pleased with himself he couldn't speak, so he gave us a very nice display of blindingly colourful lights and high-pitched noises instead.

'What's he squeaking about?' Roddy asked.

'Their fleet has to communicate, and Bert's worked out their communication carrier frequency,' Farteeta told him. 'Now they can't talk to each other without hearing us as well. It's like not being able to turn your TV off.'

'We never do,' Colin Snell said, returning with armfuls of boxes, wires and pedals. 'This is all I can find. Dad'd be mad if he found out.' But his dad was still flat out by the fence, next to Papa.

Bert's circuits flickered and glowed, and the big TV bubbled to life again. A Thregg reappeared, with his back to us. He looked round, dripping saliva and grinding his chewing-blades.

'*Fnooks* off,' he snarled. 'Can't a Thregg even take a quick *paloogle* without an intergalactic audience? Laugh while you can, you'll all be spinach fertiliser tomorrow.'

'Play something, fast!' Farteeta shouted to Susan and Roddy. Susan started playing a little tune on her flute that made the Earthling hairs on my only neck stand on end. Roddy played a lot of piano notes at the same time. I felt like I had when all of my mums swung me in the air when I was little. Colin Snell plugged in his dad's amplifiers, pressed a few buttons and some buzzes and squeals came out in a pattern that vaguely fitted the tune.

Keith, King of Threggs, made a face, snarled, then put on an evil smile. 'Unpleasant. Very. We thought we had eliminated the music plague from the Loonyverse, and then this worthless planet has to cling on to it. But not for much longer. Do you really think one feeble *footling* little flute could stop us? Or that pathetic puny piano and a music-machine we wouldn't stoop to using as a doorbell back home? You would need the power of a thousand music-machines!'

The Thregg on Keith's left nudged him.

'I mean a million music-machines!' Keith quickly shouted. 'And you don't have a million do you?

'HEE HEE HOO HOO HAH! MAYBE YOU DON'T EVEN HAVE HALF A MILLION! HEE HEE HEE! YOUR TOOTS AND FLUTES AND LUTES AND HOOTS BOUNCE OFF THE ARMOUR OF OUR CONTEMPT LIKE MISSILES OFF COSMIC SHIELDS, HA HEE HEE HO HO HO! BEHOLD, FARCICAL EARTHLINGS, THE ARMADA BEFORE YOU!'

Keith stood aside, and the screen switched to a picture of Earth viewed from the flight deck of a craft somewhere out in Near Space. From its

windows, many other craft were visible alongside –
dark, featureless slabs, each of which looked about
six Earth miles long.

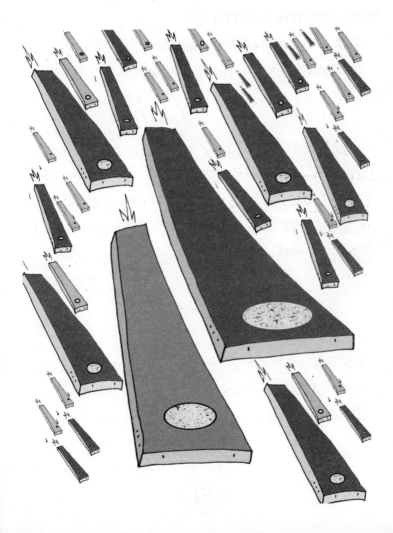

'SEE YOU SOON, EARTHLINGS! IN ABOUT SIXTEEN MINUTES! WISH US A COMFORTABLE FLIGHT! HA HA HA!'

The TV screen faded again.

But I am looking up at the dark cold sky now, Rok. The Thregg fleet will soon obliterate Earth's pathetic lonely sun. Flyzoop, our only chance of getting home, has probably been vapourised by Threggs already. There's no sign of him. This will be my last message.

Flowk

Hey Rok,

I hope you haven't organised my funeral yet, because here's what happened next.

Bert pounced on Colin's equipment with a speed that was impressive even for him. He was on to something – you could see from the way his lights flashed and his brain-cells glowed through his blue plastic skull. The thing he'd built didn't look up to his usual standard, though – he'd hitched up the replica World War Two radio he'd built on Faa (assuming then, as we all did, that

we'd arrive in 1942) to a maze of micro-circuits he'd obviously knocked up in about five milliseconds, the music machine Papa had confiscated, the transmitter of an Earth-baby alarm, and – *flaaarnnnnn!* – the *Grand Theft Spacecraft: Invasion* game. Roddy must have brought it to the party with him. Little did any of us know we'd be battling a real alien horde.

'Not fair!' shouted Roddy when he saw it. 'That's mine! Nigel gave it to me!'

'`All's fair in love and war`,' Bert rather unexpectedly snapped in his toneless metal voice. I'm always amazed by the random stuff he seems to say. Then Colin shouted 'No!' as Bert – his mechanical arms a blur of movement and sparks – stripped bits out of Colin's dad's music stuff in a flash and soldered it into the machine, dumping its control panel and pedals at Colin's feet. Then he stuck the whole thing in the input chamber of the

Improver, spun the dials, and it shot out the other end. But it looked exactly the same.

'Nothing's happened, Bert,' I said to him.

'Upgrade phase one completed,' Bert insisted, parking his weird contraption at the front of the Improver, with *Grand Theft Spacecraft: Invasion* plugged into it. His circuits glowed red, and the TV screen sprang to life again. The Threggs were still laughing, 'HOO HOO HAR'. They seem to be able to keep it up for ages and ages.

'Play into that,' Bert ordered, pointing at his strange machine. Susan and Roddy started their tune again, Colin pressed some buttons, slid some sliders and stamped some pedals. Somehow, guided by Bert's instant micro-circuitry, the *Grand Theft Spacecraft: Invasion* theme sounded as if it fitted with Susan and Roddy's tune perfectly. The Threggs laughed louder, but the head of one of them started wobbling. And then smoking. The

smoking head was laughing too, but the laughing was beginning to sound even stranger than usual. 'HEW HEW HORRR.'

Bert squeaked and whirred.

'What's Bert saying?' I asked Farteeta.

'He's saying Threggs eliminated music from the Universe because it gives them *feelings*. They can't afford to have feelings because if they did, they wouldn't be able to wipe out other civilisations whenever they needed to turn the next nice planet into a spinach plantation.'

'What's happening? What in *Klong*'s name is happening?' Papa cried. He'd finally woken up, his suckers and extenders randomly shooting in and out of his Earth clothes. I think not knowing what to do while his children, some Earthlings and a robot were locked in mortal combat with the Threggs was upsetting him. Mama, who had been waving her arms wildly to the music, rushed to his side.

Roddy and Susan were playing their tune faster and louder, but Bert's machine, playing through the Improver, was starting to make it sound to the Threggs as if there were twice as many music-machines, then ten times as many. And then a thousand.

It was the most beautiful thing I'd ever heard in my life. But not for the Threggs. They were holding their horrible heads, lurching around their flight decks and groaning.

'A thousand music machines,' Roddy squeaked. 'He said we'd need a thousand!'

'We've got a thousand, thanks to Bert and the Improver,' Farteeta said, clapping her hands.

One of the Threggs' heads suddenly exploded.

No! Looking closer, I saw that it hadn't exploded, it had dissolved and re-emerged as an equally hideous but pleasantly smiling head!

'Lay off, Keith,' it said. 'Them Earthlings'll

probably give us some spinach if we ask nicely. It'll be good for their exports.'

Bert's noises became a long stream of demented bleeps. 'What's he saying?' I asked Farteeta.

'Nothing. He's cheering,' Farteeta said, 'because the nice Thregg's got feelings!'

But the other Threggs kicked the nice one out of the way, and Keith snarled.

'RESISTANCE IS FUTILE! WE NEVER LIKED HIM ANYWAY!'

And horrors! Smoke was now starting to come from Bert's machine. The amazing dance of all the musical sounds together was slowing down. Everything was getting softer and softer, as if it would soon fade away. Bert's bleeps and warbles were losing heart. And he doesn't even have a heart. Farteeta listened closely to his fading voice.

'The Thregg boss is resisting it by sheer

anti-brain power,' Farteeta translated. 'It's creating a feedback loop that's draining the machine. Even Bert's genius is fading away.'

'Wow, an interplanetary arm-wrestle,' Colin Snell breathed.

'For the survival of Earth,' said Susan.

Then Bert's lights dimmed and everyone went quiet. Keith's demented face now filled the TV screen again. His crusty yellow eyeballs glowed, his chewing-blades glistened. As the music quietened, he began to laugh.

'HOO HOO HAR. IMBECILES! NOW YOU HEAR THE FINAL NOTES OF MUSIC IN THE ENTIRE UNIVERSE! THEN YOU WILL OBSERVE THE FINAL MOMENTS OF HUMAN, ANIMAL, INSECT, ARACHNID, AMPHIBIAN . . .'

('Get on with it, Keith, I mean, your worship!' shouted an invisible Thregg.)

'. . . **LIFE ON EARTH!**' continued Keith, pausing only to vapourise the invisible heckler.

'**HERE BEGINS THE AGE OF SPINACH! PREPARE TO MEET YOUR DOOM. AND WE DON'T DO IT NICELY, YOU KNOW. IT HURTS.**'

I looked at Susan. 'Maybe it's too late for me to take you home now,' I said to her. 'I'm really sorry. We could have had such a nice time.'

And at that moment, the loudest, craziest sound I'd ever heard ripped through the air, and only Keith's howl of rage was louder. We stood, bewildered, for a millisecond or ten. Then I looked round, and Farteeta was behind us, slashing at a bright red guitar, staring up into space with her mouth open as if she was trying to catch sight of the Threggs' fleet and swallow it at the same time.

'What's that horrible noise she's making?' I couldn't help saying.

'It's from this book Mama ordered, ' said Farteeta, playing faster and faster. 'It's nice to have a real guitar, though.'

'It's working, look!' Susan said excitedly.

Keith, King of Threggs, reeled around the Thregg mothership, his oily tentacles covering his scaly ears. Bert's invention made Farteeta's guitar shriek and whine even more. Bert's blue head brightened, and he started gibbering again.

Then there was a blinding flash, a last Thregg howl which suddenly cut off in the middle, and the TV screen went black. Bert was quiet for a moment, then the noises he made became understandable again.

'Signals terminated,' Bert said. 'Alien craft on auto-escape course. Now exiting galaxy.'

We all cheered. Mama and Papa hugged. Me and Farteeta hugged. Roddy and Colin Snell hugged. Fi Fi and Pluke werfed into the bushes. I hugged

Susan. Then Susan hugged Bert. His blue plastic skull turned pink.

Earth is beautiful, Rok. Life is beautiful. Wet blobby clouds are beautiful.

Lovely blobby clouds

Sweet little sun

Nice pointy mountains, that I have never seen

I'm sorry I was rude about the trees It is not their fault they can't talk.

Dear little oceans made of simple H_2O plus sodium chloride.

Happy flies with their cute tricks

I was just thinking this when Flyzoop crash-landed on our house.

Susan, Roddy and the Snells screamed, thinking the Threggs had returned.

I suckered Susan. Pluke suckered Fi Fi.

'It's OK, it's our spacecraft,' Pluke and I said simultaneously. 'Come back with us to Faa, please!'

'I can't leave my mum!' said Susan.

'Woofetty woof woofetty bow wow,' said Fi Fi.

'Oh no,' said Pluke. 'She's saying she can't leave our puppies!' He turned back to Fi Fi and pleaded, 'We'll take them with us, I'll teach them to whirl and zoom on Faa!'

But now Susan and Fi Fi were looking at something behind us, staring with ghastly expressions, Rok – looks I will never forget. Fi Fi whimpered and shivered, her tail between her legs. Susan stood frozen in horror, her mouth open wide.

'What's wrong, Fi Fi?' werfed Pluke.

'What's wrong, Susan?' I asked.

I whirled round, imagining Threggs were behind me.

Then I realised what had happened. Behind me were not Threggs, or humans, but three Faathings: Mama, Papa and Farteeta. Their triple doses of *Vom* had finally worn off. Their disguises had dissolved. And now Pluke was changing back into my own dear pet.

Fi Fi wailed.

My four heads shot out of my T-shirt.

Susan wailed.

There was not a drop of *Vom* in sight – Aaron Ratchet had drunk the lot.

'Susan! It's still me, Nigel,' I said, 'don't be afraid.'

But my voice had started to change back too, so that it sounded, even to me, like a ghostly roar.

How could I persuade Susan that I was harmless? The expression on her face was one of total fear. I snaked out a tentacle towards her, as gently as I could, and tuned my Faathing growl to an English whisper. 'Susan, it's all right, I'll never hurt you, please come with me.'

For a moment, I thought I'd persuaded her. She briefly put out her hand towards me then recoiled again, just as if I was a Thregg. Then, before I could say or do anything more, Bert was scooping me up in his huge mechanical arms and strapping me into our spacecraft.

'No, no! I must explain to Susan!' I cried out, but Bert is not a vast mechanical robot you can argue with.

'My children, my children!' squeaked Pluke despairingly as Bert whisked him up alongside me.

'We have to memory-blast Susan! And Roddy! And the Snells!' shouted Farteeta.

'No time, and no point,' said Papa, suckering Mama and strapping her in too. 'No other Earthlings will ever believe them if they say they've seen aliens. They never do.'

By now Flyzoop had activated the anti-matter shields, so none of them could see us any more, anyway. My only hope was to get a message to Susan somehow, so I'm going to email all these letters to her and Roddy too, before we exit Earth's atmosphere. To them, the first entry will look a bit like this:

⇆⇨⇨△ ʊ↕⇗⇨▶↘↲

↳▽ ▲△↕↘↓▽⇨⇪↲ ⇉⅂↘ ▽⇨↔⇨↓↔→ ◢↕▶
⇨↕▲↓⇨▽ ↕← ↘◢ ⇨↓↙◢ ↙↕→ ⇨↕↕⇗ ↕↔
↥↑⇨△◀↑↘

I'm going to add this message to Susan:

▽↕△△◢ ⇉ ▷⇨▽ ▽↕ △▶⇨⇨ ⇨⇨↕▶◀ ↥⇨△◀↑↘
⇉ ↙↓⇗⇨ ◢↕▶△ ⇨◢⇨⇨⇨↙↙▽↘

I hope some reader somewhere can work it out. I wonder, Rok, whether it will be translated one day and turned into one of those Earthling books I was beginning to enjoy. Roddy might be able to translate it – I think he's clever enough. He'll probably be a professor soon. Perhaps Miss Barn will read it to my class – although none of them, except Susan, Roddy and Colin Snell, will ever believe it all really happened. Bert had dismantled the Improver in about six seconds, so the only evidence of our having been here is Fi Fi's puppies. Pluke is already making plans to visit them.

I might come back with him. I'm already missing Earth. The only planet in the Universe with music. And chocolate. And jokes. And Susan.

But for now, we're heading home. See you in just ten Faa days.

Your friend in infinity,
    Flowk

Translator's note: The following fragment of paper was discovered in a small tube made of tungsten, titanium, tantalum and vanadium embedded in a matrix of cobalt. The tube, lodged in an ant hill on the Ishikari coast of Hokkaidÿ, Japan, was attracting the attention of a colony of myotis macrodactylus bats. We believe it to be the final part of Flowkwee's story.

ONE HOUR LATER: MISSION FAA

Dear Roddy,

Greetings from deep space. I hope this gets to you somehow. We have exited your galaxy and so your hopeless 'broadband' no longer works. I hope you got the letters I sent you. I'm now writing the old fashioned way and we're trying to figure out a way of sending it to Earth. I just want to tell you that Susan is on our spacecraft!

Bert scooped her up at the last minute and calmed her down

by letting her fly the ship. She did a better job than our pilot, Flyzoop, which made her happy, so it's not going to be me that tells her a newborn *fluit* could do the same.

Bert said he'd brought Susan because we needed at least one specimen to take home with us, but I think it was because he thought I'd like her to come. Maybe we were right to program Bert with feelings, after all.

But Susan isn't too happy as she's realised we're on our way to Faa and there's no turning back.

I keep telling her she'll love it on Faa, but now I understand a bit more about these things I can see that maybe she won't.

If she doesn't, I'll have to be Brave and True whatever Papa or the Emperor think and help her to come back to Earth.

Bert says I have to finish now, as we're about to enter a worm-hole that'll make all communication impossible.

Can you tell Susan's mum that she's on a spacecraft and that she's fine?

Your friend,
  Nigel

Oh Lovely Earth
Oh Earth so fair
You are a nice planet
Full of things quite rare

This is a 'poem'.
It is a song without musi
I am not very good at
but some Earthlings
are BRILLIANT at them.